MDLG Bedtime Stories Bundle

A collection of erotic lesbian age play short stories for ABDL and the Mommy Dommes who love them

By Tina Moore

Table of Contents

MDLG BEDTIME STORIES BOOK 1 1

CLAIMING TAYLOR 3

PLAYING DOCTORS AND NURSES 23

MOONLIGHT CIRCUS 39

COMIC STORE MOMMY 59

ROADSIDE BABY 79

NEW GIRL 101

NAUGHTY GIRLS GET SPANKED 119

MDLG BEDTIME STORIES BOOK 2 133

MOMMY TO THE RESCUE 135

VOTE ONE FOR MOMMY 159

BABY GIRLS GET SIPPY CUPS 177

HIGH SCHOOL REUNION.................................. 195

MOMMY WILL TAKE CARE OF IT 219

MOMMY IS MY BEST FRIEND 237

MDLG Bedtime Stories Book 1

A collection of erotic lesbian age play short stories for ABDL and the Mommy Dommes who love them

By Tina Moore

Claiming Taylor

I had seen her board the train in the morning and get off at her stop in the afternoon for months. Being a regular commuter was like that. We got to know who got on at what stop, who worked where or who only caught the train when their wife had taken the car to work. We even had a system of simple gestures to match. A faint knowing smile if your eyes happened to meet as you got off the train, the knowledge in the fact that you'd be seeing those same faces again tomorrow.

She had become a regular two months ago but from the moment I first saw her, I wanted her. I knew what she wanted by the way she swayed her hips. I knew she needed me by the longing stare she gave the other businesswomen who stood with power and certainty. With her playful bounce down the platform as she saw the train approaching and her toothy smile when she looked out the window, it was not just me who noticed her. Businessmen would shift their briefcases in front of her crotches sooner than later when she stood next to them. The jolt and surge of the train making her sway against them as she found her footing was obviously too much for them to bear.

"Here, take my seat," I heard her say to a mother of two small children. The train was particularly crowded today. It was near winter and the weather made it cool one moment and warm the next. Looking at her outfit, it was clear she was trying to be dressed for both. Her baby pink fluffy sweater was pulled tightly over her large perky breasts and the white mini skirt which she wore to match complimented her slim legs. She got up allowing the mother her seat and stumbled into a man who grabbed her arm steadying her.

"Can't have you hurting your pretty little self," he said making her pull away uncomfortably. She began to make her way down the aisle, pushing past men who refused to move, forcing her to rub against them to pass until she reached the end of the aisle. Her blonde pigtails flashed in the reflection of the window and I looked up to see her standing beside my singular seat, her purple backpack at her feet looking back up the aisle.

"I've seen you before, stop 439 right?" I ask her warmly. She looks at me, slight fear in her eyes, I wish it hadn't turned me on, seeing those big blue eyes go wide with caution.

"I get off on the last stop so I kind of see everyone get on and off. I'm Sarah," I explain holding out my hand. She looks down at my extended hand and it occurs to me that this may be the most grown up thing she's done all day. Giggling she takes my hand and gently shakes it, smiling at me like she's just told me a secret.

"I'm Taylor. So how long have you been riding the train?" She asks. Before I can answer the train comes to a sudden stop making her stumble forward, falling onto me and clutching onto my shoulder for support. She blushes when she sees her hand in my lap and takes a moment before pulling away.

"This must be a new driver today or something," she says going even brighter. I just smile it had looked so sweet her 19-year-old hand with its painted pink nails on my business skirt covered thick thighs. I laugh kindly at her attempt to excuse her hand placement and answer her question.

The train reached Central station and it filled with more people than I knew it would carry. I watched as three men pushed their way down the train to be close to Taylor, smiling like she had already agreed to give them blowjobs when they reached her.

"Hi there," one said looking at her heavy tits clad in its fluffy cocoon. She ignored him, making him turn her around to face him.

"I said hi," he said. I don't think he was expecting me to stand up behind her and give him the warning look of his life. Taylor turned back towards me and bumped into me, not having realized I was so close. Before she could say a word I took her hand, sat back down and placed her firmly on my lap. She wiggled trying to get away but I stroked her hair and whispered that it was just so those men wouldn't harass her anymore.

"Wow thanks then," she said surprised someone would come to her rescue. We talked for the rest of the hour-long commute past the city and suburbs and into the edge of the country. I learned Taylor was studying the arts at the local university and that she wanted to become a painter. I told her about my big fancy job and felt my pussy get warm when she told me she thought it was cool. The train continued to rock, pushing her against my own breasts, neatly packed away in the designer blazer I had recently purchased. I wrapped my arms around Taylor as she leaned into me and enjoyed the sensation of her resting her head on my shoulder.

"What about a boyfriend, do you have one?" I asked her letting my hand drop onto her lap, my fingers playing with the hem of her incredibly short skirt. Taylor shifted on my lap, I could have been sure she spread her legs wider as she settled in her new position.

"No, I haven't found anyone I would want to be with yet," she replied slightly pushing her pussy out. I reached under her skirt and stroked her thigh, feeling the soft crease between her thigh and her panty line. Taylor looked at me in surprise but I just smiled back at her and held her firmly on my lap by pressing my hand against her tummy.

"Um and what about you, do you have a boyfriend?" She asked placing her hand over mine as I reached up and stroked her full breast over her fluffy sweater. It made her tits look even bigger than I knew they would be, exciting me as her nipple got hard when I pull it through the thick soft material.

"No. I have no need for a boyfriend," I replied. "I prefer having a baby girl like you," I added whispering in her ear all the while groping her fluffy tits. My other hand had been resting on the top of her pussy and as she looked at me in shock by my response I slipped a finger between her thighs, feeling her warmth and her wetness against her ruffled panties.

The people who had been around us had long gone and there were only an old man and his wife three seats up as I pulled her panties to the slide and stroked along her slit making her squirm on my lap.

"Stay still for me baby girl, Mommy wants to feel you," I instructed looking Taylor in her wide eyes until she settled for me, I didn't want her bringing any attention to us. I reached under her sweater to discover she wasn't wearing a shirt, just a frilly bra which had ruffles at the front, no doubt matching her panties. I cupped one of her tits and squeezed, delighted at the feeling of her rocking on my lap in pleasure. Her nipple was hard and I pinched it making her gasp. I smiled and continued to grope her like the baby slut she was. Fingering and flicking her nipples predatorily with one hand while my other hand stroked her clit. I could feel she was close. It was hard to decide if I wanted her to cum in her panties or not, if I wanted to bring her to ecstasy and leave her sitting in her cummy panties or if I wanted to take her home with me and use her all night. I knew her stop was only one stop away as I pushed another finger along her slit. Pulling on her tits I began whispering in her ear, "Who's Mommy's good little girl. Cum for Mommy baby, make your panties wet for me." I coaxed as cum spilled from her pussy, dripped from her slit and wet her panties as we passed her stop. I smile she was mine now I didn't have to decide what I wanted to do with her I was going to do everything.

Looking around nervously Taylor realized she had missed her stop. She tried to get up but I wrapped my bigger legs around hers holding her in place as I slowly began to rub her again. I held her close to me by her tit and felt my own panties moisten at her struggle.

"It's OK baby girl, get off with Mommy at the next stop and I'll drive my sweet girl home," I told her making her calm down again. I grabbed at her breast once more, pulling up her bra making her tits bounce a few times before I took my hand from under her sweater and stroked over the top, straightening it down for her and patting her like she was my pet. I wiped her cum on the front of her panties as I took my hand from under her skirt, pulling it up to see the mess she had made. Satisfied with myself, I patted her thigh to get up and held her steady getting up behind her, taking her backpack and my briefcase in one hand and her hand with my other and led her down the aisle to the train door.

"My house isn't far," I said leading her off the platform into an alley. She was scared, I could tell but this kind of scared wasn't sexy so I stopped walking and pulled her into an embrace she eagerly accepted.

"It's OK I walk down here all the time and nothing bad has ever happened. I'll protect you little one, Mommy will keep you safe," I didn't want her to try and escape me. Taking her hand once more we continued the walk to my house.

"You're right it wasn't far," Taylor said as I led her up the garden path to the back entrance of my home. Nestled between two large trees was the door to the garage, I was hoping I could convince her to stay a little longer than she currently had planned.

We walked in and I flicked on the switch. It was my garage, but I had had it turned into a dungeon. I knew I liked it but I was glad when I saw Taylor gingerly touching the fucking machine I had next to the king size bed. Hearing my heels on the concrete she turned around quickly.

"I was just," Taylor tried to say before I pushed a pacifier gag into her mouth and groped her left breast. I kept my fingers on the gag, making sure she knew to not take it out. I took a step back and looked at her, my hands on my hips, her holding the gag in her mouth, her nipples pushing through her fluffy sweater.

"You were just what young lady? Thinking you could touch my things without permission?" I asked stepping forward and buckling the gag behind her head. I pushed her back making her fall on the bed. She was enveloped by the thick quilt and abundance of pillows, her small hands pushing them away as she tried to get up.

"No," I said sternly before turning away from her. I walked over to the glass cupboard and took out a pair of fluffy pink panties with a long slit from clit to arsehole, a white-tailed bunny butt plug and a tube of lube. I walked slowly over to where Taylor lay in the middle of the big bed, the navy linen making her outfit stand out even further.

"Take off your shoes for Mommy," I ordered placing the items down on the bed next to her. She quickly and obediently followed my command, placing her shoes neatly together on the floor.

"You have good manners little girl," I said grabbing her by her tit and pulling her forward. I grabbed at her pussy and she jumped feeling her now cold but still wet cum push into her and I laughed making her blush.

"Give me these, I have something else

you're going to wear," I instructed holding out my hand and waiting. Taylor slowly pulled down her frilly panties and handed them to me. Putting them down next to her shoes, I took the panties I had for her and slowly pulled them up her thighs.

"I know you'll like the feel of this baby girl. Mommy has everything you'll like today," I whispered in her ear as I moved the fluffy panties over her arse, lightly scratching her as they were secured. I took the lube and butt plug holding it up for her to see.

"Don't fight me on this or you'll get a spanking and it'll still go in, do you understand?" I asked as I lube the medium sized plug. I knew it would stretch her, I had chosen it for that reason. I finished lubing it and watched as Taylor nodded in understanding as I climbed on top of her and began toying with her arsehole. I pushed my finger into her and then rubbed her clit with my other hand until I heard her moan, watching as she rolled her head back in pleasure and becoming startled as she felt my finger being replace with the tip of the plug.

"Don't be scared, Mommy is here," I coaxed as I pushed it into her, enjoying the slightest whimper as her arsehole was filled with more than it was ready to take. I pushed it in until there was nothing more than the cute little bunny tail showing and rolled her onto her tummy so I could see. Every movement now caused her to moan or gasp. I pushed her down on the bed and ran my hands up the backs of her thighs stopping to grab and grope her arse cheeks, spreading them and pushing the plug into her.

"Mommy's good little princess," I said rolling her back over.

"Keep that on," I commanded seeing her reach for her sweater wanting it off. I wanted her uncomfortable and horny. I wanted her to know that I was the source of her pleasure or pain. Walking over to the fucking machine I moved it so its wide thick cock was pointing straight at Taylor's wet pussy.

"Where do you think this will go?" I teased

seeing her back up towards the head of the bed.

"And where do you think you are going?" I added grabbing her by the wrist and quickly cuffing her right wrist to the bedpost.

"What did I say about fighting Mommy princess?" I asked turning her onto her tummy and coming down hard and fast onto her arse making her yelp in surprise and pain.

"I think I said not to do it," I added knowingly after spanking her again, this time harder than before. I rubbed her arse and gently turned her around to lay on her back looking up at me.

"If it's too much let me know OK?" I asked her seriously before smiling at her and kissing her forehead. She smiled behind the gag and nodded her head knowingly.

"But I've been watching you, the way you walk, the way you talk, the way you dress in these cute little clothes teasing people with your sluty pretend innocence. You were just waiting for a Mommy to take you home and make you her good girl weren't you?" I asked taking the lube and squirting it straight onto her clit. I opened the slit of the panties and rubbed the lube roughly between her lips before pulling the machine forward. Grabbing the cock which was about to be buried in her tight pussy I rubbed the tip of it up and down her slit, pushing it slightly into her pussy. I stood up and push it over her, so that the lubed tip of the cock is above her pussy, dripping her cum and lube onto her panties. I tilt the machine down and pull her hips up, making her hold herself in position as I force the tip of the cock into her pussy, making her hold it in there.

"Ready baby girl?" I say as I turn on the machine. Taylor moans and her legs almost buckle as the cock filled her pussy. I switch it off when it is completely in her cunt and walk over to my cupboard happy with the knowledge that Taylor is stuck on the fat cock inside of her. I take a pair of nipple clamps and walking back to her, turning the machine on and watch as it exits her pussy glistening in cum and lube. It pushes back in, making her arsehole quiver resulting in her bunny tail shaking.

"Mommy likes that sweetie," I say excitedly lifting her sweater. I reach under and pull down the front of her bra and pull her tits out. I pinch her nipple as the cock rams into her making her moan and close her eyes. Opening a clamp I secure it to her nipple making her eyes pop open and a groan escape from behind her gag. I pinch her other nipple with the clamp and flick them a few times before aggressively groping her swelling tits through her sweater. I slap her tits every time the cock reaches her hilt making her hips grind rhythmically in time.

"That's it, baby," I encourage, turning the machine up watching as cum oozes out around the thick cock fucking her.
Standing up I go to my high backed armchair and sit down, watching my pretty baby be fucked, forced to cum over and over, her legs shaking more intensely with each new orgasm. I smile as I watch her cum dripping onto the sheets, making a

wet patch under her arse. Knowing she cannot take much more I go back to her bed and come up behind her. I lift her up under her armpits and move her onto my lap once more. She all but collapses into my arms and I reach down to rub her clit as another orgasm washes over her. I grab at her breasts, pulling on the nipple clamps until she yelps, causing my clit to throb.

"Last one baby," I loving say kissing her cheek as I turn the machine on faster, praising myself for buying the model which came with a remote. The cock fucks her forcefully, easily sliding in and out of her used cunt before she yells out and her legs give way. The cock comes flying out of her pussy and covers her fluffy panties and sweater in cum as it continues pumping forward and back over the top of her. I let it, I want her dirty. As she begins to breathe normally once more I turn it off and push her hips down into her mess. Her legs are still shaking and her face is flushed. I uncuff her wrists and take her hands, letting them flop down onto her tits as I place my hands over the top of hers, making her grope herself.

"Did Mommy make you cum too hard pretty baby?" I tease knowing the answer. Taylor just nods her head as she is forced to keep grabbing and squeezing her tits. She closes her eyes and rolls her head towards me and I can see her pussy still leaking cum onto her thighs. I take my hands off hers and reach under unclamping the nipple clamps. Checking the clock I see it's 8:30. *Time flies*, I think to myself as I gently unbuckle the pacifier gag. I reach for the panties and Taylor tries to lift her bottom for me but her legs buckle and give way underneath her making me laugh.

"It's OK little one, Mommy's got it," I say pulling them down off her. I take the butt plug out next and lay everything on the bed as I pull Taylor over to me and hold her in my arms.

"Did you want to go home now?" I asked stroking her check. She looks up at me and nervously touches my breasts over my blazer. I unbutton it as well as my red satin blouse and let her feel me.

"I am home," Taylor replies vulnerably making me smile knowing that I've claimed my baby girl at last.

Playing Doctors and Nurses

"There you are baby," Amanda said excitedly seeing Mindy walk into the bar. It was the monthly Kinksters mingle at a bar one of the members owned. This was Mindy's favorite night of the month when she could crawl around in the specially set up nursery at the far end of the bar and have her Mommy give her all her love. Amanda flung her arms around Mindy and took her hand immediately leading her to the area the owner had set up for the babies.

"No, you can't have that my love," Amanda told Mindy who reached for her wine. Amanda had worn Mindy's favorite outfit. A long white dress with brown knee-high boots and her hair done up in a messy bun. Mindy loved seeing Amanda, outside of these nights, she knew nothing about her. Not where she worked or what she did for fun other than treat Mindy like the most precious baby girl.

Amanda pushed Mindy gently to the padded floor and began to change her out of her adult clothes into something more appropriate for the evening. Mindy used to bring her own clothes, diapers, and toys but from the time she and Amanda had begun their relationship, Amanda had chosen what she would wear. Tonight she had chosen a yellow t-shirt with a white duck on the front and matching frilly socks. She didn't want a diaper cover on Mindy tonight and left her duck print diaper exposed for everyone to see.

"Who's Mommy's pretty little princess," Amanda cooed as she shook a pacifier in Mindy's face waiting for her to part her lips.

"I am Mommy," Mindy excitedly replied, opening her mouth so Amanda could put the pacifier in. Amanda and Mindy played all night. A few times other Mommy's came over to talk to Amanda and to compliment her on having such a well behaved baby. There were a few brats there on this particular evening and Amanda was happy

Mindy was not one of them.

"She's a good girl," Amanda said affectionately to another Mommy who was spanking her baby for not sharing the toys with the others while looking at Mindy who was making a tower out of the blocks.

As the night progressed and the Mommy's and Daddy's enjoyed more drinking, Mindy watched as one by one the other baby's found themselves bent over a knee or table taking a spanking.

"I'm a good girl Mommy?" Mindy asked fearfully. She hoped it wouldn't be her next who would be spanked in front of the others.

"The very best but if Mommy wants that little bottom of yours spanked red, that's what's going to happen, little girl," Amanda replied reading Mindy face and understanding her meaning. Luckily for Mindy, Amanda had chosen not to spank her that evening. She had felt Amanda's spankings before and knew they were not something taken lightly.

The night passed more quickly than Amanda or

Mindy would have liked and after what felt like far too soon Amanda was taking off Mindy's socks, diaper, and t-shirt and helping her get dressed in her grown-up clothes.

"I hate this part," Mindy said as she zipped up her jeans. Amanda smiled sympathetically and pulled her in for a hug.

"I know baby," she whispered patting Mindy's bottom.

Mindy woke up on the day she had been dreaming about. Today she would begin her first day at a newly built hospital as a Doctor for Oncology. She dressed in a cream-colored knee length pencil skirt with a light blue button-down blouse tucked in. Her shoes were a sensible height, a cream color which slipped perfectly over her nude pantyhose.

"Wow," Mindy said out loud as she let her thick wavy mane of light brown hair out and swayed, loosening the waves.

Mindy was inducted and filed the required paperwork before she began to be introduced to the nurses who were on her ward. By lunch, her mind was spinning and as she began to set up her office she heard a knock at her door. Opening the door she dropped the pen she was holding upon seeing Amanda stand opposite her on the other side of the door.

"I thought I taught you better than that," Amanda said in a low tone pushing Mindy to the side and walking into her office. Mindy shut the door behind her and turned around to see Amanda sitting on the edge of her desk.

"Nice," she said looking around admiring Mindy's taste.

"What are you doing here?" Mindy finally said in a hoarse voice. Amanda got up and walked to her, grabbing her by the hair and pulling it back as she had done when Mindy had been naughty at a previous meeting. It felt different her doing it now when it was just the two of them in this very adult setting.

"I work here and if you think I'm going to be taking any orders from you little girl you are sadly mistaken," Amanda replied letting Mindy's hair go.

"I was never going to order you around, Mo, I mean Amanda. I just want to do my job," Mindy answered, a little whine escaping her voice and making Amanda smile victoriously.

"Do you think you're a big girl now in your pretty office and big girl clothes," Amanda teased pulling at Mindy's blouse from her skirt. Mindy quickly rushed to tuck it back in as Amanda pulled her into her and held her firmly. She began rubbing her arse over her skirt the way Mindy loved until she stopped struggling to break free.

"Mommy is going to come in here after work baby and you are going to change into something a little bit more to my liking," Amanda said as she kissed Mindy's cheek and left the office. Mindy waited for Amanda to arrive but at 7 pm she decided to go home. Just as she was opening the door to her office, Amanda turned around the corner and began walking along the corridor to Mindy.

"I hope you weren't thinking of leaving

when I clearly told you to wait for me," Amanda said as she walked past Mindy and put her bag on Mindy's desk.

"Are you going to shut the door, or do you want everyone to see you, baby?" Amanda asked loudly making Mindy shut the door quickly hoping no one heard her. Amanda laughed and began unpacking a diaper to Mindy's horror.

"I can't do that here Amanda," Mindy hissed. Amanda walked over to Mindy, spun her around and spanked her hard on her arse.

"You'll call me Mommy here, there, every fucking where baby girl," Amanda said as she took a changing mat and powder in one hand and a diaper and pacifier in another.

"Lay down for Mommy," Amanda said as she placed the changing mat in the middle of the floor and patted it lovingly. Mindy approached slowly and Amanda reached up and pulled her by the hand to the ground making her whimper as she lay down. Amanda ran her hands up Mindy's skirt and pulled down her pantyhose until they were at her ankles. She took a pair of scissors and cut off Mindy's g-string and threw the ruined garment in the bin.

"You won't be needing this again," Amanda stated. Next, she made Mindy lift her bottom and she slid the diaper underneath her. Amanda took out a double padded wad and made the diaper ever thicker between Mindy's legs making her begin to fuss.

"Now now baby girl Mommy knows what you need," Amanda said as she pushed a pink pacifier into Mindy's mouth and snapped her fingers at her angrily as she tried to take it out. Submitting, Mindy kept it in and began sucking on it as she fought to not enter her baby headspace. Amanda put extra powder on Mindy and fastened the diaper in place pushing it into Mindy who squirmed. She then took the pantyhose and rolled them back up Mindy's legs, pulling them over her puffy diaper securing it in place. Amanda rolled down Mindy's skirt and enjoyed watching her fight herself as a big thick puffy diaper was locked in place over her grown-up skirt.

"That's more like it baby," Amanda said looking at Mindy who still had a pink pacifier in her mouth.

"I know just the person who would like to see this," Amanda said as a knock came from the door. Mindy's eyes went wide and she tried to stop Amanda who only grabbed her by the hair and pulled her back. As Amanda opened the door, Mindy was stunned to see the director of the hospital standing there looking at her. The director was in her mid 50's and her mean stare and womanly body made Mindy excited and nervous at the same time.

"You said you had a good girl, but I hadn't realized she would be so easily babied," the director exclaimed locking the door behind her.

"You can call me Auntie Lisa baby Mindy. I'm going to have some fun with you," the director said slowly unbuttoning Mindy's blouse. Mindy looked from Amanda to the director and was lost as to what to do. Before she knew it her blouse was on the floor and so was her skirt and heels. The director had tied her wrists behind her back and was pulling up a frilly pink skirt over Mindy's large diaper. Even with the pantyhose squishing it down, Mindy's diaper exaggeratedly stuck out from the rest of her. The director sat on the floor and Amanda pushed Mindy down, making her fall on her face and letting out a whimper of pain.

"Oh did the little baby hurt herself?" The director cooed picking Mindy up and laying her upwards across her lap. Mindy slowly nodded her head, feeling herself seep into her little headspace. Amanda noticed it too and came over with Mindy's favorite blankie snuggling it into her face. Before Mindy realized she had the director's womanly breast in her mouth and was being rocked as she nursed.

"She likes that," Amanda said looking at Mindy's fluttering eyes.

"She'll be asleep soon and milk will spill from her pretty mouth, here," Amanda added handing the director an extra cloth to mop up

Mindy.

"That promotion you put in for. You just got it," the director said to Amanda who kissed Mindy's head.

"Thank you," she replied walking to the door leaving Mindy in the arms of the director and her mouth full of her milk.

Amanda was right, she is a sleeping girl, the director thought as she felt Mindy's body become heavy with sleep. The director had already planned for Mindy to start a week later her coming in today was solely for this. The director dressed again and knowing the ways out of the hospital which would cause the least attention, she picked up Mindy and carried her to her car.

When Mindy was all buckled in, the director turned the car on and began the drive to her house.

"Where am I?" Mindy asked as she sleepily woke up from the bumps on the road. The director put her hand on the front of Mindy's diaper and rubbed it lovingly.

"You're alright baby girl. Your Mommy and I have decided I will look after you for one week and she will look after you every other week. We know how much you love being cared for and now you can be cared for more than a few hours a month," the director explained pushing on Mindy's bladder making her squirm. Mindy hadn't realized Amanda would take her complaint about leaving the bar quite so far.

"But I have to work, you hired me!" Mindy said as she continued to squirm under the director's touch.

"You'll be starting next week baby girl. Then you'll be changed and fed and come home with me for a week and the following week you'll do whatever your Mommy wants you to do. Don't bother complaining about it, the decision has already been made," the director sternly replied pinching Mindy's nipples over the pink long sleeve she had dressed her in while she was asleep.

"Here we are baby," she said pulling into a dark garage and closing the door before getting out. The director came around to Mindy's side and let her out, taking her hand and leading her inside. Mindy's diaper was so thick she had to waddle and the director loved seeing her new little girl have to waddle fast to keep up. The director brought Mindy to a room which made her gasp. She saw a cot and a changing table, a locked fully enclosed cage which had a padded floor and stuffed toys, a toy box and a rocking horse which had a pair of hand and ankle cuffs attached to it.

"Do you like it, little girl?" The director asked as Mindy dropped to her knees and crawled into the room. She began looking through the toy box and found a big soft yellow duck she dragged around the floor with her by the wing. The director smiled as she watched Mindy touch the cage nervously.

"That's where naughty babies go. You're not a naughty baby are you sweetie?" The director asked coming over and opening the cage door, laughing when Mindy quickly crawled to the other side of the room and shook her head. The director pulled Mindy to her feet and led her to the rocking horse.

"You're going to play here while I sort out some dinner alright baby," she explained as she cuffed Mindy's wrists and ankles to the horse and used the remote to make it start rocking. Mindy was surprised it had come with a remote. She was also surprised at how narrow the place to sit was. As the rocking horse moved forward and back Mindy could feel the narrow piece of wood between her legs push into her diaper and rub her pussy. Before long the motion of back and forth has separated Mindy's pussy lips and her clit was being forcefully rubbed along the diaper as she rocked. The director came back into the room and watched as Mindy was made to cum by the rocking horse and smiled seeing her nipples go hard and her hips grind down into her diaper.

"It looks like someone is enjoying themselves," the director said as she watched Mindy cum for the fifth consecutive time.

"It feels so good Auntie Lisa," Mindy replied

making the directors own clit begin to tingle.

"Come on, you've had enough now. We are going to eat dinner," the director instructed turning the rocking horse off and uncuffing Mindy. She helped Mindy down and patted her diapered bottom a few times as she led Mindy into the living room.

Mindy was placed in an adult-sized highchair and fed dinner, then taken to the bathtub and washed before the director changed her diaper and put her in pajamas.

"You are just the sweetest," the director said fastening Mindy's purple mittens with a lock on her wrists. Mindy had never worn these before and they felt strange. She shook her hands seeing if they would come off but they didn't.

"Baby, do you really think I'd make them loose enough for you to get them off?" The director laughed seeing Mindy's attempt. She put Mindy in the cot and locked her mittens to a chain which was connected to the cot.

"You're not going to go anywhere little girl.

You're mine for a week and I plan to keep it that way," the director said as she tugged on the chains making sure they were securely in place. The director turned off the lights and shut the door as Mindy clapped her hands as she saw the glow in the dark stars that covered the ceiling.

The weeks passed just like the director had said. For the week Mindy was the director's baby and for every other week, she was Amanda's. During the day she was the new Doctor with an impressive office and had many a male nurse flirt with her and by night she was diaper-clad and breastfeed. It wasn't the life Mindy had thought she would have for herself, it was better.

Moonlight Circus

Mia loved the circus. Ever since she had been taken by her mother when she was 6 years old she knew the circus is where she wanted to be. Fast forward twenty years and after a lifetime of gymnastics and strict dieting, she was ready.

Mia had seen them advertising with their signature marketing style, a series of chalk graffiti around the city with their emblem. She had jumped at the chance and had taken a taxi to their performing tents in the showgrounds. Captivated by the dark blue and silver stripes of the big top, Mia nervously had approached a woman sweeping the entrance.

"Hi, I'm looking for Madam, I'm here about your advertisement," Mia said hoping the woman would be helpful.

"Oh really, what do you do?" The woman asked placing her broom to the side and smiling at

Mai.

"I'm an acrobat," Mia replied feeling silly as she had said it with such enthusiasm. The woman giggled and gestured for Mia to follow her into the tent.

As they passed through the tent Mia tried not to look star struck as she saw other people performing. There were body contortionists and other acrobats performing at heights Mia had never attempted, she hoped she wouldn't have to audition with them watching.

"Madam," the woman politely called as she knocked on a red wooden door.

"Enter my darling," came a flamboyant voice from inside. The woman turned the intricate brass handle and held the door open for Mia who took the hint and walked inside. Closing the door behind her, Mia turned around to see the woman had gone.

"So you have come about the job," Madam stated more than asked. Mia took in her form. She had clearly been some sort of dancer in her youth. She moved with an elegance and grace Mia had not seen before, her slender body almost snaking its way around her as Madam circled Mia.

"An acrobat," Madam said stepping back and looking at Mia.

"Yes. How did you know?" Mia said excitedly. Madam shook her head and put her finger to her lips.

"I ask the questions. You, my little acrobat merely answer them," Madam replied. Mia nodded and moved from one foot to another.

"You may show me now," Madam instructed expectantly. Mia snapped into life and remembered why she was here in the first place. *She's mesmerizing,* Mia thought as Madam led her to the performing floor.

Mia auditioned as though her life depended on it. She wanted this job yet she felt a strange feeling of not wanting to disappoint Madam, a woman how had hardly spoken to her whom she had met a mere ten minutes earlier. As Mia performed she felt Madam's eyes on her the whole time, taking in her form, her positioning, the way she landed and her connection to the audience who had stopped what they were doing and come over to watch her.

"She's perfect," Madam stated turning off the music.

"You may stop," she added as Mia turned to see why the music had stopped. Mia slowly made her way back to the group who waited for her below. She had thought it was strange that Madam was the only one out of the 6 people she counted who was standing. The others were sitting at her feet, one woman even cuddling her leg as she leaned against her.

"Bravo Mia," Madam stated as she clapped purposefully. Mia blushed and looked around the tent relieved to see the others smiling at her.

"Thank you, I hope you liked it," Mia replied.

"I liked it very much. Enough to offer you the opening position, you will start tomorrow night." Madam instructed.
Mia practically skipped home. I impressed Madam!

She thought to herself. And I also got my dream job? She said questioning herself as to why she was more relieved that she had proven herself to Madam than get the job she had worked so hard to become a professional in.

Mia woke up early the next day, still in a haze from the previous day. She got ready and felt like she was floating on air as she entered the big top. Madam had told her to come and see her first thing when she arrived.

"Good morning my sweet one," Madam gushed seeing Mia. She embraced her and Mia had to force herself not to melt into Madam's arms as she was held longer than Mia usually hugged a person. Breaking the embrace Madam took Mia's hand and showed her where she would change and told her that rehearsal was in 30minutes.

"I hope you are ready, I want nothing but you're absolute best. Think yesterday but better," Madam instructed as she left Mia to change. Coming out into rehearsal Mia was greeted by the other performers. She spun, flipped and twirled until she thought her body could take no more, and that's when Madam told her to do it all again. She made them do full performance rehearsals back to back for 5 hours and at 4 pm she finally called out stop.

"Very good, come here," she instructed the group of 6 acrobats who formed a line one behind another. Mia was confused as to want was going on but she joined the queue, annoyed she was pushed to the back.

"No, let my new baby come to the front," Madam ordered making Mia confused. The other acrobats turned to face her, the one who had been first in line smiling encouragingly. Mia slowly walked towards Madam who had her arms wide open. Her chestnut hair flowed over her firm breasts and Mia swallowed hard when she caught herself looking wantonly at them.

"Tonight is Mia's first performance. If anything is going to go wrong it will be tonight and I need all of you to make it look like it was meant to happen," Madam said as she rubbed Mia's back. The others just stood there nodding in agreement and where dismissed.

"Mia," Madam called when Mia was almost about to exit the tent. She turned around and saw Madam gesturing for her to come over to her. Reluctantly, Mia began to walk to Madam who silently took her hand.

"I want to make sure your muscles will not be too sore tonight. Come," Madam ordered. Mia was taken to Madam's caravan and instructed to lie down on her bed.

"Take them off," Madam said nodding to Mia's training tights. Slowly Mia rolled them down but she was too slow for Madam who began to pull them down to her ankles to hurry her up. Madam reached for Mia's panties and Mia resisted, trying to push Madam's hands away.

"Shh silly girl," Madam cooed. She took Mia in her arms and managed to have Mia bare arsed within a moment.

"There," Madam stated in satisfaction.

"What are you doing?" Mia said softly. Madam looked at her and frowned.

"I thought I told you I would be the one asking the questions," she replied.

"You cannot break my rules. I'm hurt you do not trust me. Have I not been lovely to you?" Madam asked.

"Yeah you have but, this?" Mia questioned. Madam stood up and grabbed Mia's arm pulling her onto her lap and spanking her arse before Mia knew what was happening.

"Stop fussing little girl, you will learn to trust Mommy. Take your punishment like a good girl," Madam ordered sternly spanking her arse again. Madam covered Mia's mouth and continued to spank her until her arse was red and blotchy. Each time her strike feeling more intense than the last Mia stopped fighting and lay limb over Madam's lap. When she was finished, Madam stood Mia up.

"There are three hours before we open, try to be a good girl until then," Madam instructed passing Mia her panties and tights and leaving her to get changed.

Mia didn't remember how her first performance went, her mind was still on the spanking, how Madam referred to herself as Mommy and how everyone seemed to know Mia had been spanked. *Had they heard? Does this happen a lot?* Mia asked herself as she was given the fourth sympathetic look in a row. One of the other acrobats had even left a bottle of lotion on top of her bag with a note saying she might find this useful.

As the last of the tidying up was done Mia found herself alone. She had been told by Madam to stay after the show, even though Mia wasn't living with them yet she still needed to be a part of the end of show celebrations. She walked around the tent wondering where everyone was as she hears Madam call for her. Mia made her way to the room where she had received her first spanking and froze when she arrived.

"Come in baby," Madam said. She was

surrounded by the other performers, all 9 of them. Some were drawing, some were watching a movie and eating popcorn and some were reading. What they all had in common was they were in diapers and wearing baby clothes. The pictures they were drawing were with crayons, the movie they were watching was something Mia watched when she was younger and the books they were reading were picture books. Madam smiled as she saw Mia take it all in.

"Well baby, are you going to come to Mommy or not?" Madam asked patting her lap. Mia looked around the room again and felt herself move towards Madam. She opened her arms and sat Mia on her lap, giving her a blankie to hold onto.

"You may call me Madam by day sweet darling, but after the show my name is Mommy. If you choose to stay with us, you will be my littlest baby and I will love you so. Your brothers and sisters will play gently with you and Mommy will make sure nothing bad happens to you. Would you like that my little one?" Madam asked in a loving tone that made Mia finally melt into her arms. Knowingly, Madam took a pacifier and wiggled it between Mia's lips making her giggle.

"I thought so," Madam stated in satisfaction. She stood up and took Mia to an empty corner of her caravan and snapped her fingers to the floor.

"Down baby," Madam instructed watching as Mia sat down. Madam took a diaper and a white shirt, pink terry toweling dungarees and matching socks. She pushed Mia to the floor and smiled at how compliant she was.

"Mommy's going to change you every night sweetheart, once the show is over, you're my sweet baby girl in her sweet baby clothes again," Madam stated while peeling Mia's clothes off. Powdering her for the first time made Mia sneeze and the woman who Mia had met on the first day, Tiffany, waddled over to where she was laying,

"The movie is finished Mommy," Tiffany said sitting down next to Madam who was now rubbing her hands over Mia's diaper-clad pussy.

"Alright honey. You need to let Mommy finish dressing baby Mia first and then I'll put on another one. Have you and Sammy decided what you want next?" Madam asked to see Tiffany shaking her head. Madam kissed the top of Tiffany's head and patted her bottom as she crawled back to where the TV was. Madam then took the white shirt and wriggled it over Mia's head followed by the dungarees. Finishing it off with her socks, Mia was surprised when Madam effortlessly picked her up and carried her through the caravan. She held Mia on her hip while she put on another movie and sat on the long black couch and bounced Mia on her lap.

Madam decided she wanted a tea and getting up she had put Mia down on the floor to play with Tiffany and Sammy. Sammy had played puppets with her making her giggle and clap her hands excitedly and Tiffany had shown her the sticker book Madam had bought her the previous week. As Mia became sleepy, she crawled over to Madam who was reading with one of her other babies and

Mia reached out for her.

"Oh is someone tired?" Madam asked knowingly. She had put Mia through the rigorous rehearsal before the show deliberately she had been waiting for this. Mia nodded and sleepily rubbed her eyes.

"Yes Mommy," Mia replied as she climbed onto Madam's lap to hear the end of the story. When the story was over, Madam instructed that she would be back shortly and that when she came back everyone was going to sleep. She didn't wait to hear the reply as she lifted Mia onto her hip again and carried her into the bedroom.

"You will sleep with me every night little girl," Madam stated pulling back the sheets. She gently placed Mia down who nodded in agreement. As she settled into Madam's big bed, she touched her diaper making Madam laugh.

"That stays on baby girl," she explained. Madam pushed Mia's hands away as she rubbed the diaper through her fuzzy dungarees.

"Why do you think I keep you in them, baby

because you'll wet yourself if I let you take it off. Baby girls can't have big girl panties," Madam cooed. Mia pouted and looked away.

"That's right baby girl, Mommy fully expects you to have a full wet diaper in the morning. You don't want to make Mommy cross again, do you? Let's have a practice now, I have a sneaky feeling you need to wet your diaper. Come on sweetheart, Mommy will change you after," Madam coaxed feeling Mia through her dungarees and diaper, feeling for them to become warm and full. Mia tried to refuse but Madam pointed to the cane on her bookshelf.

"Trust Mommy when I say you don't want to feel that on your pretty little bottom sweetheart," Madam said making Mia instantly wet her diaper. She began to cry and Madam smiled enjoying the power she had over her. Madam began to sing to Mia, soothing her with soft heartfelt rhythm as she changed her.

"Mommy's clean baby," Madam stated patting Mia's new fresh diaper. Madam had made this one particularly thick, forcing Mia's thighs to remain open, exposing her diaper-clad pussy. Madam rubbed her and sung her to sleep, turning the light off and shutting the door quietly behind her.

Mia woke the next morning before anyone else. She lay next to Madam who had dressed in just a singlet and shorts and snuggled into her smiling when Madam pulled her in and held her tight.

"Good morning little girl," Madam suddenly said making Mia happy she was still Madam's baby.

"Good morning Mommy," Mia replied. Madam opened her eyes and smiled at Mia.

"The sun is up my darling. Once that diaper is off and you are in your big girl clothes, don't get caught calling me Mommy, understand?" Madam stated lovingly but there was a warning in her voice nonetheless.

"OK Mommy," Mia replied, sad it would be over shortly. As if reading her mind, Madam reached down and rubbed her pussy tenderly.

"Don't worry baby, it's only for a little while. Every night you'll be Mommy's special little girl. But both shows must go on," Madam explained reassuringly.

Madam continued to rub Mia's pussy and began to make her grind herself down on her hand as Madam cleared her throat and raised an eyebrow expectantly. Mia gave her a puzzling look before remembering she needed to wet her diaper. She was relieved Madam didn't spank her again for forgetting as she filled her diaper making Madam smile and close her eyes as she fell back asleep leaving Mia to lay in her wet diaper for another hour.

As the months went on, Mia became accustomed to her daily routine of training and performing and nightlife as Madam's baby. Enjoying the freedoms of the adult world during the day, and happily let Madam treat her as a baby by night. Madam had a way of making her feel like she was the most special of them all but Mia was careful not to show it, she was pretty sure the others felt the same way she did. Madam had that way about her. She could walk into a room of one hundred people and have each of them leaving with the feel of being the only one in the room.

When a newspaper journalist asked her why the Moonlight Circus was the most famous Circus in modern history she just laughed and said, "We are a family." She had read that out to everyone over breakfast making half of them laugh and the other half choke on their food.

"A family, how very poetic," Tiffany said as she buttered her toast.

"Yes a family, with you Madam at the head of this very close family," Sammy added making even Madam laugh.

"Well I had to make it somewhat entertaining, she was incredibly dreary," Madam said defensively smiling at Mia. Mia smiled back but looked down at her breakfast.

"What is it, Mia?" Madam asked sensing something was wrong.

"Nothing," Mia lied, making the table become silent. Madam walked to where she was sitting and bent down to meet her eyes.

"Mia," Madam said warningly. Mia looked around and felt her face begin to blush. She pulled up her skirt and Madam saw her diaper was still on.

"Yes, because that's what babies need Mia," Madam explained. Mia looked at her inquisitively unsure of how to form her question without making it a question. Sammy looked down and suppressed his laugh, he had learned the hard way not to laugh at his adult baby brothers and sisters.

"Oh Mia, come on then," Madam finally said seeing Mia's embarrassment. She stood up and took Mia by the hand, lifting Mia's skirt to show the table the front of her diaper.

"The baby doesn't want to be Mommy's baby any longer," Madam stated. Mia pulled away but Madam's grip was firm.

"Maybe I wanted you to be my baby a little bit longer today Mia? Hey, did you think about that? Now that the tour is over, maybe I wanted you in diapers during the day as well," Madam explained as she rubbed the front of Mia's diaper in front of everyone making her blush red. Tiffany stood up and came to stand next to Madam.

"Can I be in diapers during the day as well please Madam?" Tiffany asked. Madam took a step back in shock.

"You must want this pretty bad if you are willing to be spanked just for asking," Madam said as Tiffany nodded yes.

"Very well we have three weeks until we move to another city and begin the next tour. If you are in my caravan by the time that door shuts, you can be my baby until we move out," Madam said laughing as she picked up Mia and watched as the others ran to her caravan door.

Comic store Mommy

Jessie had been coming to the comic store around the corner from her apartment ever since she and James moved into the neighbor. James had thought it was silly, Jessie had never even read a comic let alone owned a collection of them. He would tease her when she went out to the weekly comic book club meeting stating that he couldn't believe she would rather spend her evening with a bunch of loser virgin nerds than spend time with him. Jessie would stay silent during his taunts, knowing that staying in and spending the night with him would mean laying on her stomach as he took her from behind, pounding her pussy with his chubby cock and full, hairy balls with monotonous repetition until he cream pied her hole and began in her arse until that too was dripping with his cum. She never came. How could she when he thought foreplay was titty fucking her and finishing in her mouth?

When she had tried to show him ways to gently touch her clit or to lick her pussy but he hadn't been interested, continuing to use her as his personal cum whore. The comic book club was her night off from being fed his cock and pumped full of his cream. Her night where Sally would make choc chip cookies and hot tea, where the people would be interested in what she had to say and make her feel like she belonged to something important.

She wanted to leave home early, telling James the group had something important to discuss.

"Well, you know what's waiting for you when you get home," he started pulling out his already hard cock, lifting her skirt and rubbing it up and down her panty clad arse crack.

"James!" Jessie exclaimed pulling away and grabbing her bag. As she bent over she felt him again at her arse, hands groping under her skirt, pulling her arse cheeks apart and feeling his fingers push her lips open. *Great*, Jessie thought in discontent feeling him tap his cock against her panties. He lifted the side of her panties and placed his cock underneath. Jessie felt the wet pre-cum rub against her arse cheek as he grabbed her by the hips and rubbed his cock on her bare skin.

"James I have to go," Jessie said pushing his hands off her hips.

"Shh," James replied wrapping an arm around her waist, using his body weight to bend her over and stuck his thumb in her mouth. Jessie tried to use her tongue to push his big thumb out of her mouth but it was held in place by his hand which was firmly squeezing her face. He eventually took it out of her mouth and reached under her skirt once more, taking his cock out from under her panties and pulling them down in one quick motion. Still bending her over and holding her still with his other hand he guided his cock into her pussy and stuck his thumb up her arse.

"You're not going until those panties are wet with my cum. I want those fucking nerds to know you're mine." He stated aggressively as he pounded her from behind. Jessie stopped struggling, she knew she would be late but what could she do? James had her bent over, her pussy full of his cock and his thumb in her arse. He took his hand from her waist and grabbed her arm and pushed her against the front door. Jessie knew he was close, she could feel him cumming inside of her. As he reached his climax he pulled out and held his cock over her panties, covering them in his load. Some of his copious thick white cream fell onto the floor but most filled Jessie's panties. Jessie felt his thumb pull out of her arse and jumped when she felt him pull her panties up. His hand cupping her from the front and from behind. He rubbed her cum loaded panties firmly on her pussy pushing them into her cunt and arse. Jessie could feel his cum drip down her thighs. She was definitely going to be late now, her bus would have already be gone from the bus stop and another one would be another ten minutes. James wiped his cock on her arse cheek, wetting the outside of her panties.

"Have fun tonight," he said as he pushed her out of the house and quickly shut the door behind her. Jessie didn't have a key, James had said she didn't need one because he worked from home and would always be there when she finished work. She knocked on the door wanting to change her panties but no answer came. She stood there, thinking about the choc chip cookies, warm tea and people who made her feel valued but she mostly thought about Sally. Sally with her kind smile and loving manner, the way she would gently play with Jessie's hair every time she greeted her. Deciding she didn't want to miss out on that she headed towards the bus stop.

"Oh, I was beginning to think you couldn't make it!" Sally exclaimed jumping up from the circle and rushing to greet Jessie at the door. Jessie smiled Sally was wearing her favorite dress, the green and white poke-a-dot one that showed her ample cleavage. Sally's green eyes complimented the dress and her long red hair made her look like a vision.

"Yeah sorry, I missed my bus," Jessie replied not exactly lying. Sally took Jessie's hand and led her to the group, grabbing a cookie and pushing it into Jessie's mouth before turning back to lead her to the circle. Jessie giggled as she took the cookie from her lips and bit down happy they were still warm. She found her seat and shifted uncomfortably as James's cum squelched into her tender holes. Sally gave her a questioning look making her blush and she quickly looked away hoping to curb her curiosity.

The meeting ran like clockwork, she shared her thoughts about the recent comic book they were reviewing, the character development and the storyline. All the while aware Sally had hardly taken her eyes off her. As the meeting ended, Jessie waited until she was the last one still sitting in the circle. She didn't want to run the risk of someone seeing the wet patch on the back of her skirt she could feel was most definitely there. She got up as

Sally walked someone to the door, grabbing her bag and trying to push it behind her to cover her skirt.

"What are you doing?" Sally asked startling Jessie, she hadn't realized that Sally had been watching her from the door.

"Getting ready to go home?" Jessie replied unsure of what the correct answer was. Sally locked the door and walked over to Jessie, she looked down at the bag she was pushing behind her and looked back up into Jessie's eyes.

"Have you had an accident?" Sally asked wondering what Jessie was doing. Sally had seen Jessie's panties under her skirt during the meeting, as she was sitting directly opposite her and had noticed the clear change in color indicating that she was definitely wetter in some places than others.

"What no!" Jessie exclaimed taken aback. Sally thought for a moment before grabbing Jessie's bag making her gasp in shock and blush in shame. Sally reached around to Jessie's bottom and gently patted her over her skirt.

"Well, whatever it is, I can't let you leave like that. Let's get you cleaned up," she stated taking Jessie's hand and leading her out the back. Jessie knew James would be waiting for her. She knew that she was due home in 15 minutes. She was hoping whatever Sally had planned it wouldn't take too long.

Sally opened the office door and put Jessie's bag on the couch before leading her through another door. The room was dark and Jessie held Sally's hand tighter nervous about being surrounded by blackness.

"It's OK Jessie, Sally is here, I'm going to take care of you," Sally said in her loving southern voice. Jessie felt Sally push her down onto something soft and lay next to her. She felt Sally hold her in a way that James never had and she sighed contently albeit involuntarily when Sally began to stroke her forehead.

"I thought you might need some loving little one, I hadn't realized you needed it so bad," Sally said getting up. Jessie quickly felt for her, grabbing her arm and pulling her back down.

"It's OK I'm just going to get you something. You'll be alright here for a moment," Sally explained reassuring. Sally waited until Jessie let go and got up. When Sally came back she kissed Jessie's cheeks before reaching under her skirt and pulling her panties down.

"I'm just going to wipe you, clean baby," Sally stated wiping a wet wipe over Jessie's pussy before cleaning her thighs, arsehole, and bottom.

"What happened baby girl?" Sally said taking off Jessie's skirt, happy Jessie was so willing.

"James," was all Jessie could say as Sally sat behind her and rocked her in her arms.

"He fucked me and came in my panties, making me wear them here if I wanted to come tonight, he wanted people to know I was his," Jessie said as she began to cry. Sally was glad the room was pitch black, she wasn't sure Jessie would have been so honest if she had been looking directly at her. Sally kept rocking Jessie, feeling a tear fall on her arm she reached up and stroked Jessie's cheek.

"Are you really his?" She asked seriously, hoping for an encouraging answer. Jessie shook her head and Sally smiled victoriously as she enjoyed Jessie's head making her tits shake.

"Would you like to be mine? I would treat you a lot better than he would. I bet even if you say no he keeps going. If you ever said no to me we would stop immediately and we'd cuddle and I'd kiss forehead until you felt better," Sally said turning Jessie around and feeling for her hand. Sally placed Jessie's hands on her breasts.

"I've seen you staring at them baby girl," Sally revealed making Jessie gasp and blush.

"Would you like to taste them?" Sally asked.

"Um, I don't know, isn't that weird or like," Jessie tried to say as Sally pulled down the top of her dress and ran her nipple over Jessie's lips.

"Open your pretty mouth for Mommy Jessie," Sally lovingly ordered. As Jessie gasped, Sally pushed her nipple into her mouth.

"Suck it baby girl," Sally gently instructed, pulling Jessie onto her lap and began nursing her. Jessie sucked as she was ordered and quickly swallowed Sally's milk as her mouth was made full.

"Good girl Jessie. Be a good baby for Mommy," Sally cooed stroking Jessie's arm and patting her bare bottom while she nursed. Sally took a soft blanket which was folded next to her and wrapped Jessie in it feeling her skin becoming cool. Jessie snuggled into Sally, holding her full breast and making Sally's milk rush her mouth, softly cooing as she sucked.

"There's my good girl," Sally whispered bending down to kiss Jessie's forehead, enjoying the feeling of her breast being relieved of its heaviness.

Suddenly, Jessie remembered the time and pulled away from Sally, breaking their embrace.

"I have to go, James will be mad I'm so late," Jessie fearfully stated feeling around trying to find the exit. Sally put her breast back into her dress, only slightly annoyed the other one hadn't been milked as well and took Jessie's hand.

"Darling, you deserve better than him," she stated as she handed Jessie her skirt back.

"Will you be OK without panties? Those ones are too dirty baby," Sally asked lovingly.

"Yeah it'll be fine," Jessie replied as she put her skirt back on. Sally led Jessie to the door, opening it and blinding both of them for a moment.

When Jessie's eyes adjusted she turned around to find Sally standing in the doorway of the room they just exited. She looked past Sally and saw what looked like a baby playroom. There were blocks and toys in a toy box, soft pillows, and blankets where they had been laying and a double size adult cot. Jessie turned to look at Sally who smiled and closed the door behind her.

"What was that?" Jessie asked innocently.

"Mommy's playroom baby," Sally replied honestly.

"I saw um, diapers and stuff," Jessie said

looked around the ground. Sally reached behind her and opened the door again.

"You would have, would you like a closer look?" She asked Jessie who began to blush. Jessie bit her lip and her breathing became shallow as she just nodded.

"Say please baby," Sally coaxed, not wanting to push Jessie too far but wanting her to submit.

"Please Mommy can I look at your things," Jessie replied, giving Sally more than she thought she'd get. Sally pushed the door open further and Jessie walked past her, almost perplexed. Sally watched as she slowly made her way around the room, touching pillows and toys, running her fingers over a stack of diapers and looking at the collect of pacifiers.

"I use to love this book!" Jessie exclaimed. Sally smiled and walked over to where Jessie was standing.

"You probably still do," she replied taking the book and reading the cover. Jessie looked at her waiting to see what she would do next.

"You use to love these too, and I bet just like this book you'd love them still," Sally said picking up a diaper and raising an eyebrow at Jessie who just blushed.

"I don't know," she said looking down to her feet, seeing her bare pussy remembering she wasn't wearing any panties.

"Well how about this, let Mommy diaper you and then you can sit in my lap while I read you this story?" Sally questioned. She looked down at Jessie who was shifting from one foot to the next nervously.

"We don't have to Jessie," Sally began to say before she was cut off.

"No. I mean, yes, I mean," Jessie stammered making Sally laugh.

"What do you mean little girl?" Sally chuckled.

"I want to try, I just haven't done this before," Jessie said looking nervous.

"Then give Mommy your hand and come with me," Sally replied lovingly as she took Jessie back to the pile of blankets and pillows in the middle of the room.

"Lay down sweetie," Sally instructed as she gently lifted Jessie's hips and slid the diaper underneath her. Jessie played with Sally's hair as it tickled her face when she leaned across Jessie and reached for the powder. Sally sprinkled the powder over Jessie who began to suck her own thumb.

"Aren't you the sweetest," Sally exclaimed securing the diaper firmly around Jessie's waist. Sally sat back and patted her lap and Jessie crawled to her and snuggled against Sally's ample chest as she began to read the story.
Jessie had almost fallen asleep when she jolted upright and looked at Sally fearfully.

"It's too late, I really have to go," she said reaching down pulling off her diaper. Sally tried not to get upset by the sudden change in dynamic and put the story to the side and handed Jessie her skirt. Jessie looked at her skirt and then looked down at the diaper she had almost taken off longingly.

"You said you had to go?" Sally reminded Jessie who looked up, clearly unsure of which she preferred.

"What should I tell him?" Jessie asked. Sally smiled, I told you-you needed Mommy little one, she thought to herself taking Jessie's hand and leading her to the front door.

"Tell him I kept you late because I needed help packing up and everyone else left before I had the chance to ask them," Sally suggested. Jessie smiled, she liked that Sally was true to her word, that if Jessie wanted to stop, things stopped. She liked that Sally didn't try to keep her or make her break up with James.

"Oh, I was thinking of telling him, that I'm leaving," Jessie replied with a cheeky smile. Sally gasp and wrapped her womanly arms around Jessie almost smothering her in love and affection.

"But can you please come with me. I'm a bit scared," Jessie asked.

"Oh, of course, I am coming, Mommy is not

letting you go near that monster without her," Sally stated protectively. Jessie lunged forward and kissed Sally on the mouth taking her by surprise. She smiled into the kiss and wrapped her arms around Jessie once again breaking the kiss to look at her in her eyes.

"There will be rules with me baby girl, I'll give you all the loving you could ever need but you've got to be a good baby for Mommy. I will give that little bottom of yours a spanking if you are naughty. Do you understand?" Sally explained sternly. Jessie nodded her head which was followed very quickly by a, "Yes Mommy."

Jessie nervously knocked on the door and was startled by its almost immediate opening.

"Where the fuck," James began to growl stopping as he saw Sally. Sally saw Jessie change from her excited, bubbly playful little girl to a downtrodden neglected and abused woman in an instant. She was happy she had come with Jessie, she needed her.

"Hi, I'm Sally. You must be James," she stated reaching out to shake his hand. James reluctantly shook her hand but was still blocking the entrance.

"I'm leaving you," Jessie suddenly said in a whisper. James looked at her and then looked at Sally and back to Jessie.

"You're what?" He aggressively stated. Jessie reached for Sally's hand who offered it to her instantly. She looked up at James, the man she had let use her for years and repeated what she had said, "I'm leaving you." James lunged for her but Sally stepped in and pushed him back making him fall on his arse. Jessie was surprised by Sally's strength and reached for her arm cuddling onto it. Sally enveloped Jessie and turned her away from James so she couldn't look at him.

"Make a scene and I'll call the cops," Sally stated plainly.

"In fact, you can fuck off while I get her things," she quickly added walking Jessie past him. She left Jessie in the hallway as she went back to

James who was still sitting dumbfounded on the floor. Sally grabbed him by the ear and threw him out of the house shutting the door behind him. He thought about banging on the door but believe Sally when she had mentioned the police so he just waited quietly outside.

"Come on baby, show Mommy what's yours," Sally said holding Jessie who had began to cry. Jessie walked into their bedroom and found her big travel bag. Sally went to the cupboard and took out Jessie's clothes and neatly folded them, placing them in the bag. They took her toiletries and laptop, books and the homewares she had bought. When they had collected everything of Jessie's, Sally turned around to find her standing naked behind her.

"You're going to need some clothes little baby," Sally said admiring Jessie's lithe little body.

"I know Mommy, but I don't want to take these ones with me," Jessie replied pulling on a pair of baggy jeans and a cropped top. Sally looked at the bed where Jessie had left her cum soaked panties and skirt in a pile on top of James pillow.

"Good girl," Sally said walking over to kiss her forehead and take her hand.
James didn't say a word as Sally opened the door and led Jessie away from him.

"I was worried he'd start up," Jessie said sighing with relief as they hailed a taxi.

"No one messes with your Mommy," Sally whispered to Jessie before she gently pushed her into the taxi, happy to be taking her baby girl home safe and sound.

Roadside Baby

I saw her standing there on the side of the road looking lost. My truck is so high set that I quite literally saw her coming a mile away. She was standing there, kicking up the dust and playing with a stone, kicking it around in her pink high top sneakers. The road is a long and lonely place and this particular strip is known for having working girls but something about her made her look out of place. It was the way she didn't even bother looking at the trucks and cars that passed her, the way her denim overalls hung in an innocent way rather than a sluty one. As I drove closer to her I saw she was holding a blue teddy bear by the ear and I smiled at how pretty her blonde hair freely swaying in the hot breeze was.

"What are you doing here baby?" I asked as I pulled up and pressed the window down. I must have startled her because she backed away but with nowhere to run on this barren dusty stretch of road she didn't go too far. When she didn't reply I opened my door and jumped down. She was clearly surprised to see a woman driving that huge rig because her eyes sparkled in astonishment. She walked back over to where she had been previously standing and smiled down at her feet.

"I don't really know," she replied softly. By the looks of her, she was no working girl. She couldn't have been older than 22 by the fullness of her skin and the lack of lines around her eyes. She looked me up and down, taking in my ripped denim offcuts and white trucker singlet under my opened red flannel shirt. I'd rolled the sleeves up revealing the bottom half of my two fully tattooed sleeves and work boots.

"So, you don't know why you're here? Are you lost? Are you waiting for someone?" I asked taking a hair tie and tying up my own long blonde hair in a loose ponytail. She turned to look up the never-ending stretch of road.

"I come from the town up there but I'm

never going back," she said looking at me plainly. I was at a loss as what to do. I knew what I wanted to do but even though she held her teddy bear, I wasn't sure if it was something she'd want to do. I'll admit, I had made a couple of working girls my babies over the years on long nights when I was lonely. The easiest money they'd probably ever made but I couldn't just pay this cutie to call me Mommy and then kick her back out onto the street. For one thing, she didn't belong there.

"Well, I'm headed down that way. I've got a 74-hour trip I'll be making if you want to come with me. No funny business I swear," I said making her giggle.

"I don't have much money, but you can have what I've got if you take me," she replied. Oh, I wanted to take her more than she knew, take her out the back of my cab and rub my nipple over her pretty lips and feel her tonguing them as I rocked her. I composed myself long enough to reply in a timely manner stating, "No you keep your money, I'm not about to take money from a baby." She laughed and thanked me as I helped her into my truck. I put her backpack with everything she owned in my cab and jumped into the front seat, turning up the song on the radio and pulled out back onto the road.

We had driven in silence for about half a mile before she spoke. She'd been looking out the window and taking quick glances at me. I pretended not to notice, I could tell she was worried I'd try something with her.

"I like your nails," she said softly. I looked at my newly French manicure and smiled.

"Thanks, baby. Maybe we can find a nice place to get yours done," I replied making her sigh contently closing her eyes.

She hugged her teddy as the truck rolled on and was soon asleep. The rocking of the truck can do that to you, especially if you're not the one driving it. I pulled into a truck stop as the night began to get late and got out, making sure not to wake her. I'd learned her name was Becky and that she was in fact 22. She was the youngest of 7 and her parents had been violent abusive drunks. I'd found her after her father had kicked her out of the house because she wouldn't give him money to buy drugs. Apparently, Meth was their new drug of choice.

I walked into the diner and ordered two steak sandwiches and two chocolate shakes, not the healthiest meal in the world but it would have to do. I walked around the shop attached to it looking at postcards and other crap they sold while I waited for my order. Looking out at the dirty window back towards the truck I thought about Becky in her cute outfit hugging her teddy as I felt my pussy begin to get wet. As my order was called I shook off the feeling and went to pay. I had hardly taken two steps outside when I felt Becky's arms wrap around me in a tight embrace taking me by surprise.

"I thought you'd left me," she said almost in tears. I put the food down and hugged her back, involuntarily kissing the top of her head, relieved she didn't seem to mind.

"I just went to get some dinner baby. It's OK, Mel is here," I replied soothing her. I could feel her heartbeat pounding fast in her chest as she pressed into me. It had taken all my strength to say Mel and not Mommy and I was somewhat impressed that I had managed.

"Will you help me carry this back?" I asked her giving her a job to make her feel important. She nodded yes as I handed her the paper bag with our sandwiches.

"Good girl," I stated as she carried it back to the truck.

We got back to the truck and I put her back in the passenger seat while we ate. I buckled her in nice and tight and enjoyed her small tits bouncing as I pulled on the seat belt making sure it was secure.

"Why are you a truck driver?" Becky asked as I handed her half of her sandwich. I half choked on my shake, laughing at her question.

"Because I wanted to be one?" I replied unsure of what she was trying to say.

"Yeah but you're so pretty and you have

this whole cool, edgy, bad girl but really nice thing going on. You could have worked in an office or something," Becky said wiping her hands clean. I saw she missed a spot on one of her fingers and took a napkin in one hand and leaned forward to take her other hand in mine and began wiping her fingers clean as I replied.

"Becky, just because I'm pretty and edgy and cool or whatever else you think I am doesn't mean that I can't also be nice and caring. And as far as an office goes, I would hate that. I love the road I love the openness of it. I love that it let me meet you for example," I answered honestly. I loved that she hadn't pulled away from me when I wiped her clean I think she liked being care for.

"What do you like most about me Mel?" Becky asked. Hearing her say my name made my stomach knot itself in delight. I knew what I wanted to say, that I loved that she was clearly a little baby who needed a strong loving Mommy to take care of her, but I chose something more generic.

"You're lovely to be around and you're not rude," I settled for. Becky clearly wanted a better answer than that as she scoffed and rolled her eyes at my response.

"You could say that about a dog," she teased making me laugh.

We finished our food and I took her to the showers to get ready for bed. There was only one shower which worked and I was surprised when she pulled me in with her and locked the door behind us.

"We are both girls," Becky giggled. As she began to take off her clothes I tried so hard not to look at her youthful body. Sure she may have thought I was pretty, but my 38-year-old body looked not a day younger. She turned the water on and it splashed on her perky tits making her small nipples hard as I passed her the body wash. I looked at her and knew I would have given anything to wash her pretty skinny body, feeling her pussy mound in my palm and rub shower gel over her back. When she realized I was still fully clothed she giggled and began to help me take off my clothes which only made me raise my eyebrows.

"I'm helping," she said sweetly and I let her look at my heavily tattooed body as I undressed.

"It's like a story," Becky said paying attention to my chest tattoo. She gingerly ran her fingertips over my flesh making me shiver which made her very impressed with herself. She giggled and turned back to the water as I took off my pants and joined her. As we washed she spun around playfully and stood facing me, her mouth and my nipples the same height. I had had my boobs done five years earlier and their fullness looked wonderful so close to Becky's face. We showered in silence, except for Becky's playful giggles as she splashed in the water. By the time we got out, it was late and I knew we needed to get to sleep if I was going to make the journey in time.

"But I'm not sleepy Mel," Becky playfully complained as I pushed her into my bed. She wore little short shorts that showed the start of her bottom and a singlet without a bra making her nipples hard and easily visible. I had chosen my usual cotton knee length boxers and a baggy t-shirt, bed was meant to be comfortable.

"It doesn't matter if you're sleepy or not Becky, we are going to sleep now," I said with a slight seriousness to my voice she hadn't heard before. She quietened down and was asleep before me, which I found funny for a person who was not sleepy 10 minutes earlier. As she slept I stroked her hair lovingly and gasped as I saw her begin to suck her thumb. It was all too much for me to not pull her close and kissed her forehead making her smile in her sleep. I had thought about replacing her thumb with my nipple but chose to just hold her through the night.

I was just beginning to drift to sleep with the beautiful Becky in my arms when I woke to something wet and warm pressing against my leg. I yawned as I woke up to see Becky was also waking up, however far more terrified than I was.

"What is it, sweetie?" I asked becoming

concerned by the look on her face. Becky didn't reply to me, she just bit her lip and began to shed silent tears I looked down to see she had slightly wet the bed. The front of her pajama shorts was soaked through but luckily the thick 1000 thread count sheets had saved the mattress.

"Oh, baby. Did you have an accident?" I asked rubbing her arm affectionately.

"I'm so sorry Mel I don't know what happened, you've been so nice to me and I've just ruined everything. I'll go, you probably don't want to see me again," Becky said as she pulled away from me and stepped back.

"Stay right there," I said in the voice I would usually save for when a baby was naughty, but I wanted her attention.

"I'm not mad at all baby. I should have known, the teddy, the giggling. Why didn't you tell Mommy you were little and needed a diaper for bed?" I ask taking a gamble. *It can only go two ways,* I said to myself as I looked at Becky who began to blush.

"I thought you'd think it was weird. You're so cool, I didn't want you to laugh at me," Becky said looking at her toes which she was curling up.

"I don't think you're weird little girl, I think you just need a Mommy who will love you. Can I be your Mommy sweetheart?" I asked her as she looked up in delight.

"Oh yes please Mommy!" Becky exclaimed jumping into my lap now ruining my pajamas. I laughed and hugged her back, kissed her cheek and began to strip the bed. I threw the sheets in the dumpster and took her hand leading her to the showers once again. This time she waited for me to take off her clothes and I put them in a pile as my earlier fantasy played out. I took her in one arm and held her close to me as I washed her lithe little body. I rubbed her body until she was in a thick soapy lather and then guided her under the water to rinse her off. I sat on the small ledge where we had placed our new pajamas and put her on my lap. She wrapped her arms around my neck as I spread her legs with mine and used the water as lube to play with her pussy. I could feel she was tight as I toyed with her pussy hole, pushing just the tip of my finger into her making her gasp and press her chest into mine.

"Don't forget to breathe baby girl, Mommy isn't going to hurt you," I coaxed reassuringly as I pushed my finger knuckle deep into her making her take it. I kept my finger in there as I rubbed her clit gently with my thumb and kissed her pretty lips. I loved that she had moaned as we kissed when I began pulling my finger out of her just to ram it back in, this time with more ease as she began to moisten. I fondled her arse cheek as she was gently finger fucked and held her as she came in my arms. Deciding she had had enough I cleaned her once more and put on her pajamas. This time, I had chosen what she was going to wear. I had a stash of adult baby clothes and diapers in my cab for those times I wasn't interested in being denied and I had chosen a blue singlet and a white diaper cover for Becky. I was grateful it was so late as I took her into the change room, and quickly diapered her. Seeing how cute she was diapered for me I had half a mind to make her go topless, but remembering there was a world outside of the doors I held up her arms as I pulled on the singlet. Next, I pulled up the snuggling fitting diaper cover making her diaper press into her pussy. That's how I like my little ones, cunt dripping and begging to be fucked and having a diaper rub on your pussy all night will have that exact effect.

"Up you come," I said picking her up and carrying her to the door. I quickly carried Becky back to the cab of my truck and made her sit on the floor while I put on new sheets. I patted the bed and enjoyed watching her struggle to climb up into bed with her thick diaper and reached down to pull her up. She cuddled into me and I patted her padded bottom until she fell asleep contently in my arms as I pushed my nipple into her mouth and fell asleep to her nursing.

Becky became my trucking baby. I had a car seat

made for her which could lock her hands by her side and her legs cuffed at the ankles for when I wanted unrestricted access to her. Those were some of my favorite times to fuck her. When she was diapered and held down I would place a vibe in her diaper on her clit and reach my hand down her diaper to rub her pussy until she made my fingers wet with cum. I'd thread the chain of her nipple clamps through the finger hole of her pacifier and make her suck for hours which made her clamped nipples bounce with each suck and bump in the road keeping her horny. I kept her with me 24/7, looking after her and making sure she was entertained. I knew some of the other truckers liked kinky play so I took her to their puppy play nights and got drunk with the puppy owners as I watched her play with their puppies. Life was grand. There was just one thing I hadn't got to do to her yet, and that was punished that cute little arse of hers. She'd been so good, she did exactly as I told, she let me fuck her when I wanted and how I wanted, she had let me exhibit her in her diaper to anyone I wished. What was also great was that she had happily traveled over the country with me. There was not a rule she had broken or a bratty remark she had said. But I still wanted her over my tattooed thighs until her bottom shone red. I had decided I would try and make her get in trouble. She knew she was not allowed to say no to me, saying red she knew was fine but no was a different story altogether. I had decided to take her to a playgroup with other babies to see if I could trick her into saying no.

We approached the house where a Daddy Dom friend of mine was hosting a baby play day and Becky shifted nervously in her car seat.

"What if they don't like me, Mommy," she asked fearfully. I looked at her and knew they would like her.

"Who are you worried won't like you baby girl? The other babies or their Mommy's and Daddy's?" I asked as I turned the engine off. I looked at her and waited while she clearly thought about her response.

"Both. What if they think I'm not good enough or something?" Becky said making me laugh.

"Oh baby, the will love you," I replied opening the door and walking around to her side. My friend lived on a huge property so I had dressed Becky in a large diaper without a cover, happy I didn't have to conceal it. She had a pink dress with white teddy bears on the collar and when she bent over even slightly her big thick diaper was on full display. That's how I liked her, on display.

"I'm so glad you could make it!" My friend Michael exclaimed walking out the door and greeting me warmly. He bent down and looked at Becky in the eye, making her reach for my hand.

"Well aren't you just the dearest. You must be Becky, you can call me Sir," Michael stated reaching out to pull the front of Becky's dress up. She squirmed and leaned back on me as Michael touched the front of her diaper.

"My little angel has this exact type on. I can

tell you two will be friends," he stated patting her pussy before turning around and walking inside. Becky tugged on my hand as Michael turned his back to us and whispered in my ear, "Mommy, do I let people touch me today?" God she was such a good girl always wanting to do the things I wanted. I took her two hands in mine and kissed them.

"Yes baby, if a Mommy or Daddy wants to touch you through your diaper you let them today alright?" I asked her. I could tell she didn't want it, I hoped she would say no at some point today. We walked inside and Becky was introduced to Angel, Michael's baby girl and the two of them played with dolls in the living room as one after another more babies joined them. I got compliments at how well Becky played with others and how good she was. At one point a Mommy of a boy who was showing Becky dinosaurs came up and made her sit in her lap and she did nothing to resist as the woman patted and rubbed her pussy while rocking her for an hour. As much as I was having a lovely time, nothing had made my heart sing as much as when I finally heard it. Becky had been drawing with Angel who had drawn over her picture. It was a picture of me and her holding hands. Becky had come up to me crying and showed me the drawing holding it up for me to see. Angel had then come over and told me what Becky had scrunched up her drawing and a mortified Becky turned to me and when I began clarifying the situation she had interrupted me saying, "No!" I smiled and stopped talking and Becky's eyes went wide with the understanding of what she had just done. She knew better than to interrupt me and she also knew better than to contradict me.

"Game over little girl, come with me," I said as I took her wrist and lead her to the couch. A few other Mommies joined us and they watched as I pulled down the back of Becky's diaper and struck her for the first time. She yelped and began to cry as I slapped her arse time after time. Telling her what she had done wrong and how disappointed I was in her. She begged me to stop telling me how she would be good again and not make the same mistake twice. As her bottom became a nice rosy red I change from slapping her to spanking her. For me, the difference is in the intensity. A slap is a sting, a spank is a thud that sends something to a little's brain telling them to shut their mouths and that's exactly what Becky did. She shut up and took her spanking until I felt her go limb in surrender to me. I rolled her over and looked into her eyes and knew she had reached her limit. Lovingly, I applied lotion to her arse and gave her her blankie from my bag. I lifted my t-shirt to let her nurse and kissed her forehead until her tears stopped flowing.

"You're lucky to have such a nice Mommy. When my little girl is bad, she gets a spanking and then sent straight to the corner," one woman said. "You are such a softie on her Mel!" Michael said bring me a beer. I knew I wasn't 'soft' on her, I just knew what her little limits where and when I'd pushed her far enough.

"When Angel is bad, she gets tied face down and fucked in the arse while I spank her," he added I'm sure making Becky grateful she wasn't Angel. I smiled and stroked Becky's hair and patted her tummy.

"I don't need to do that to my good girl, she hardly does a thing wrong," I said looking down at her lips around my big nipple and her thumb gently rubbing her own cheek with her blankie, full of pride Becky was mine.

New girl

"You can't live in there!" My sister exclaimed upon seeing the apartment I had just bought. Sure it wasn't in the nicest part of town but it was no means unlivable. The building was 80's dated but fitted with the basic modern luxuries, the trump card was it was close to the cinema where I had recently been promoted to manager.

"It's pretty nice inside," I said defending my new home. It was my first piece of real estate. No more renting and dealing with shitty landlords, no more having my food stolen by housemates, just my own little haven from the world. She wouldn't understand. My sister Molly had married the rich boy in her high school class when they graduated college and had never actually worked a day in the career she studied four years for. She had become pregnant the day she graduated and I'm pretty sure her husband had purposefully kept her that way for the last four years. But I didn't want to live like that. I wanted freedom, even if it meant having to struggle for a while and settle for something less than glamorous, at least it was mine. I continued to drive Molly home and helped her out of the car she was pregnant with baby number 5. I held her up as she made her way up the mansion steps and to the front door. Their maid opened the door for her and began gushing and fussing over her so I said goodbye and walked back to my ten-year-old beat up car. It looked so out of place in contrast to this grand old family home with its perfect gardens and water features. *At least it's mine,* I said to myself driving away.

The cinema gig was fun. I got to eat all the popcorn I wanted and had tried every combination of soda you could think of. The other people who worked there and I made fun of the customers after the shift as we cleaned up and I had already busted three couples fucking during a screening. All in all, it was a lovely, routine, basic life. That was before I met Abby. She was the daughter of the owner of the cinema and had begun working with us because her father thought she needed to 'understand the principle of hard work'. When I had heard this I rolled my eyes but when I was then told I would be the one who would have to educate the princess in 'hard work' I really lost it.

"I bet she's never worked a day in her life," I told one of my colleagues as we swept the floor. He wasn't listening I could tell.

"I heard she's really hot, Bell," he replied proving he wasn't listening to me. I just huffed and thought miserably about the next shift which would be with her.

True to her word she showed up on time the next day for her first shift. I was instantly annoyed with how beautiful she was. Her shoulder length choppy cut blonde hair had its ends dyed pink and she stared at me with the greenest eyes I had ever seen. It made me feel quite ordinary with my brown hair and brown eyes. She smiled sweetly when I asked her to restock the candy bars and count the straws. She didn't really need to count the straws, I just thought it would be fun to make her. I showed her how to use the register and pour the soda so it wouldn't overflow. As the night progressed I was even more annoyed by the fact that she wasn't a bitch. I had hoped she would be Daddy's little rich princess but she was down to earth and didn't even hesitate when I told her to clean the restrooms.

"So how did I do?" She asked me while sitting on the counter while I swept under her feet. She had that flirtatious voice that had driven every guy she had spoken to mad with lust. At one point I had to get a guy escorted out because he was holding up the line and became aggressive when I told him to leave. She was bad for business but stunning to watch.

"OK, I guess. I mean, it's only your first shift so I can't really give you a verdict yet," I said as she jumped down and took the broom from me.

"I can do this for you Bell," she said

smoothly. Hearing her say my name made my heart flutter. *No, just fucking no*, I told myself knowing what that meant. There was no way I was going to be another one of those stupid people drooling over her. I handed her the broom and walked away, pretending that the posters needed straightening.

"You're like a grumpy Mommy you know, Bell," I heard her say loudly. I'm glad it was just the two of us left, hearing her say Mommy made my cheeks blush.

"Well, there are things that need to be done and the longer it takes the longer we have to work," I replied defensively making her giggle. I turned to see what she found so amusing putting my hands on my hips.

"I didn't say it was a bad thing," she replied.

"Look, Abby, just finish up there so we can leave," I answered not amused by her games.

Our shifts continued with her teasing. She had called me this kind of Mommy and that kind of Mommy for weeks and I had even realized I'd come to expect it from her, sad when she didn't call me a Mommy and wet with desire when she did. Hearing her call me that, and only me that made me wonder what kind of girl she really was. I decided I had nothing to lose trying to find out.

The next shift I did the usual clean up routine with her and waited patiently for her taunt.

"Gosh Bell, I can't believe you are such a bossy Mommy," Abby said without turning around to look at me. I was glad she didn't because she didn't see me open a lollipop and walk up behind her. I grabbed her arm and she jumped, shocked to be handled so roughly. I pushed the lollipop into her mouth and held it there while I looked her dead in the eyes.

"Then do what I tell you to do and I wouldn't have to be so bossy, little girl," I assertively stated turning around and walking away again before she saw my face burn red. My mind was racing. I could not believe I had just done that, I could not believe my pussy was wet as I spoke to her like a naughty little girl. I hoped she would be cool with it, I mean, she had been calling me Mommy for weeks. As I was having a nervous breakdown I felt a tugging on the hem of my shirt. I looked down to see Abby, sitting on the floor and looking up at me.

"I'm sorry Mommy," she said, melting my heart with her big green eyes and candy red-stained lips. I didn't know what to do, but something came over me as I knelt down and cupped her chin in my hand.

"Abby. When we are at work, Mommy needs you to be a good girl and tidy up fast. We don't want to be here all night, little girls like you need to be tucked up in bed, not walking the streets because you played too long after work," I found myself saying. This time I didn't blush, I practically swooned. This 19-year-old doll wanted me to be her Mommy. Me a 27-year-old uni drop out who lived in an average part of town doing a less than average job for under minimum wage, I couldn't believe it. But I was sure as shit not going to pass up having a girl like Abby in my life. She nodded her head and put her lollipop back in her mouth and I held out my hand and lifted her up. We exchanged numbers and as I walked to my car, Abby came running over and kissed me full on the lips.

"Night night Mommy," she said as the moonlight glimmered in her eyes.

"Sweet dreams little girl. Mommy will see you tomorrow," I replied wanting more than anything for the next shift to start.

"Hello?" I said answering the office phone. Abby was meant to be here twenty minutes ago and I must admit I was worried.

"Mommy, it's me," Abby replied, she sounded scared.

"Where are you? Are you coming in tonight?" I asked her kindly sensing her distress.

"My car broke down and I can't get there, I thought about walking but it's so dark and I'm scared. I didn't who to call," Abby said in one breath.

"You didn't think to call your parents? Or a pickup truck?" I asked her wondering how many brain cells she had underdeveloped due to being babied her whole life.

"My parents are in France. No, I didn't think to ring a pickup truck, what if the guy is all touchy feely, I've seen movies, I know what they are like," Abby said trying to prove her knowledge.

"You know nothing little one. Message me your location, I'm coming to get you," I replied making her whimper at my harsh comment. I felt my phone vibrate in my pocket and I put her location in my GPS and told her to stay where she was. I told the staff they would have to work without me tonight, that I had to pick up Abby and the guys offered to come with.

"No, she doesn't like or want you. Stay," I instructed confidently as I walked out the door and towards my car.

As I drove to Abby's location I wondered what I would do when I got there. Would I take her to work, would I ring the towing company to get her car, would I take her to my house? Maybe we would go to hers? As the thoughts ran through my mind I saw her car on the side of the road. She was right, it was dark. I was hoping she would be in the car like I had told her and happily surprised when I saw her head turn around and behalf blinded by my headlights, I got out of my car.

"Heard you need your Mommy little girl," I stated as I opened her door. Abby jumped out and flung her arms around my neck making me stumble backward.

"I was so scared, anything could have happened," she hyperventilated.

"But nothing happened and you're safe with Mommy, come on, come and sit in my car while we ring the tow company," I said reassuringly to her taking her hand and leading her to my car. I turned the heating on, she was clearly in shock from the one thousand percent non-scary event she had just experienced, to try and calm her while we waited for the tow truck.

"It's nice in here Mommy," Abby cooed as

she cuddled with me on the back seat. I looked at my car and looked at her confused.

"What do you find so deeply appealing about it baby girl?" I asked brushing her hair out of her eyes.

"It has you," Abby quickly replied as if knowing the question I was going to ask. She began to stroke my stomach and slowly made her way up to my breasts, giggling as I looked down on her and saw her toying with my uniform buttons.

"Come here little one," I said lovingly as I moved her over my lap so she was snuggling into my neck. I pulled her close and moved my arm under her and began rubbing her back with my hand as my other one unbuttoned my blouse.

"This is what you want sweetie?" I asked in a soft low tone watching her nod in response. I pulled down my bra and let her see my breast as I took her hand and carefully placed it on the top of my tit, enjoying how she stroked it and pulled it out looking for my nipple.

"I would have never of guessed you would

be so sweet little girl," I said in astonishment as she began to kiss and lick my nipple. I pressed her head against me as my other hand reached for the button on her short denim shorts. Unzipping them, I saw her cute pink checkered panties and stroked her over the top of them making her moan softly against my nipple. She stayed there, my sweet girl in my arms, her pussy being gently caressed. I slipped her shorts off her and rolled down her panties, happy she was so obliging. I was gentle with her as I spat in my hand and rubbed her already wet pussy with my palm, gliding my fingers down her slit and entered her without warning making her gasp and clench her pussy tight around my fingers.

"It's OK baby, let Mommy have you," I said as I began to softly finger fuck her. She nodded and I felt her pussy slowly loosen giving me unrestricted access. I wasn't interested in making her cum, tonight I just wanted to feel her. Feel her heart beat against mine, feel her wetness and her hot breath and tongue as she sucked on my nipples.

After a while I felt her go heavy in my arms as she drifted off to sleep and remembering the tow truck could be here any moment, I gently shook her awake.

"Baby, you can't fall asleep just yet," I whispered making her stir. She opened her eyes just as the headlights of the truck came beaming around the corner. Glad I woke her in the nick of time I buttoned my blouse and got out to greet the trucker.

"You been here long?" He said as he hoisted the exotic car into the trailer.

"Long enough," I replied smiling sweetly. I didn't want to get into a conversation with him. I wanted my baby back in my arms. As if reading my mind Abby came and leaned into me, hugging me and turning away from the man. She dipped her head and I felt her shallow breathing on my exposed chest just under my neck. The tow man noticed and tried hard not to look as I wrapped my arms around her making her feel safe and protected. I didn't care if he looked, but there was no way he would be touching her.

He secured her car in no time at all and I told him the address where to drive it. He offered Abby a lift home but told him I would take her and I was thankful when he left it at that and drove away.

"What a night," Abby said walking back to my car. I unlocked it and buckled up her seat belt, kissing her cheek as I walked around to the driver's side. I turned the engine and began to drive to my place. I had made the decision on what she would be doing tonight.

"Are you taking me to your house, Mommy?" Abby asked as we passed the cinema.

"Yes baby," I replied placing a hand on her thigh and squeezing it slightly.

"I just have to stop into the store and pick up something first. You're going to wait in the car while I go. I know you'll be alright," I added pulling up to the corner store. I got out and Abby didn't say a word, she just watched as I left.

I had already ordered diapers online but I hadn't

bothered to order powder because I hadn't thought this would be happening for some time. I found the one I wanted and took it to the counter happy the woman didn't ask me any questions. I got back to the car and passed Abby the powder making her eyes go wide.

"All babies need their bottoms powdered before they get diapered," I explained to her which made her gasp and giggle nervously.

"I actually haven't ever gone that far before Mommy," Abby said looking up at me nervously. I smiled at her, I couldn't figure out if I should tell her it would be my first time too or if I should act like I had a clue about what I was doing.

"It's going to be really nice Abby. Mommy is still learning as well. If it's too much we can stop baby. I'm not going to hurt you," I assured her as honestly as I wanted to about my own skills. Seeming pleased with my response Abby turned the radio on and sang every song the rest of the car ride home.

I parked my car in the garage and took her hand

leading her to my door. I turned on the light and Abby walked in and looked at my things inquisitively. She walked to the window and looked out over the city.

"You have a really nice view," she stated. I was somewhat aware she hadn't called me Mommy or used her cute little baby voice and I wondered if she was as nervous as I was.

"Is this alright baby girl?" I asked her taking her to the living room and laying her down on my new black leather couch. It was cold on her thighs and she squirmed around lifting her legs off the material.

"Yes Mommy," Abby replied. I smiled and told her that we could stop at any time, that it wouldn't be fun for me if she wasn't having fun too. She jolted upright and wrapped her arms around my neck and whispered, "Thank you," in my ear making me delighted she felt so comfortable and safe with me. I took off her shorts and panties easily, making sure to put a blanket under her bottom so the cold wouldn't touch her.

She lifted her bottom and I playfully patted it as I placed the diaper underneath her and pressed on her hips to lower. I let her take in the sensation of the diaper before I opened the bottle of powder and sprinkled it over her making sure to use enough to stop any chaffing but not too much to make it messy. I fastened the diaper in place and looked down at her, surprised at how my life had changed in the last two months.

"Does it look, silly Mommy?" Abby asked snapping me back into reality.

"No baby girl, you look adorable. Let me take off your big girl top and put you in something comfier though," I said lifting her shirt off her and replacing it with a jungle themed long sleeve.

I took her into my bedroom and we cuddled until we fell asleep, my last thought being, *She's not Daddy's little princess at all...she's Mommy's.*

Naughty girls get spanked

There were two things in the world that I knew. One was that I loved learning how to make money, and the second was that I hated people. They just got in the way with their bullshit lives and lack of motivation to change their situation. That's why when I turned 21 the first thing I did was buy a block of land in the middle of the woods. I had gone to college the following year and let people use the land to keep their cattle while I studied, earned and saved money. I thought it was a better idea than spending it on going out with people who couldn't go one sentence without mentioning the latest celebrity and their makeup line. So while they partied and vomited up their guts, I stayed in and worked on my primary skill online marketing. It didn't take too long before I was earning enough to pay off my student loans and I began saving for the house I was going to build on my land.

Within four years I had made my first million dollars and I took half and had my dream home built on the huge acreage. I maintained my online marketing business and comfortably worked from home for the next 3 years. Life was great. I no longer had to deal with the outside world and their bullshit. However, I was lonely. There wasn't anyone particularly interesting in the one shopping strip town I lived in and I didn't really want to be down there enough to be considered a local. So I decided to advertise for a house cleaner. I thought if I'm going to have to be around someone they might as well be doing something to help me.

I had to wait 6 months before I met her. Lana. The woman who swore to me she was American but her very clear Russian accent made me wonder. It honestly didn't bother me though because she had my place looking divine.

"You need to tidy these things," Lana said moving my washing out of the way. I looked over my computer to see her folding the clean washing I had sitting on a chair for the last three days. She had a point so I just smiled and looked back at my computer.

"Did you hear me?" Lana said in an angry tone. I shut my computer lid down and looked at her shocked she would speak to me like this.

"You work for me Lana, not the other way around," I said getting up and knocking the neatly folded laundry to the ground and walking back to my computer. Before I reached my chair she had me by the arm and was pulling me back to the front of my desk. She bent me down and kept me pinned by her forearm and spanked me hard for the first time.

"You naughty girl. Making naughty things. When I clean you not make mess," she said as she spanked me over my jeans. I struggled to break free but she just kept spanking me until I gave up. I thought it would be over then but she turned me around to face her, undid my zipper, pulling my jeans down roughly making me sway forward and back. Turning me back around she pushed me over my own desk and spanked me again and this time I really felt it. She took my panties in her hand and pulled them up into my arsehole and spanked my arse until I could feel its warmth making my face burn red.

"You not make mess now yes," Lana said turning me around and sitting me on the desk making me look at her. I had never been so embarrassed. In my whole life, I had never had someone spank me or pull my panties the way she did. What was worse was that I could feel that my panties were not only in my arse but that they were wet. I had enjoyed this. I nodded to Lana who just huffed and walked out of the room. Something came over me and I quickly dropped to the floor and began tidying up the mess I had made. The marketing adds I was working on could wait, I didn't want Lana to be even madder at me.

The memory of Lana spanking my arse stayed with me for days. Probably because the sting that now greeted me every time I went to sit lasted for days. I had slept on my stomach for the following few days and had made sure that the house was tidy when Lana was due to work the following week.

As she walked around my house I followed, showing her the things she didn't need to clean rather than showing her what she needed to clean. I couldn't tell if she was impressed or not. Her deadpan face made me nervous as she went from room to room and inspected it.

"You learn lesson fast," Lana said making me filled with pride. More pride than I wished it had as I blushed bright red and looked at my toes when she turned and saw.

"You like?" She asked. I wasn't sure what she meant so I looked up, still blushing.

"I like what?" I asked in the politest tone I had. She gestured a spanking and I flinched making her laugh.

"Good girls need no spank," Lana explained taking my hand and leading me to my bedroom. I had assumed I'd forgotten to clean something or put something away when she pushed me on the bed and had half accepted that a spanking would occur. But I was surprised and very wrong when I turned around to see her standing at the edge of the bed with a toy cat. I frowned slightly unsure of what was going to happen when Lana climbed up onto my bed and pulled me into her arms. I let her, remembering how strong she was and how much I didn't want to be spanked. She pushed the toy into my arms and took each of my hands and made me hold it.

"Play," Lana ordered. I looked down at the toy and wondered what she meant. It wasn't an instrument, and I hadn't played with toys since I was a kid.

"Don't be bad girl, I say play," Lana said repeating herself. I took the cat and moved its paws along the bed hoping this would satisfy her. Luckily it did and she left the room leaving me confused and unsure of what was happening. As I got up to follow her out of the room she came back through the door and snapped her fingers in my face.

"No. Bad girl. Lana say play and Katie play,"

she said making me jump back on the bed and play with the toy cat. I looked at it and had to admit it was cute. It was brown with a white tummy and green eyes and a long soft tail. I played and Lana watched until she reached into her bag. She pulled out a magazine and sat on the end of my bed while I played with the cat, snapping her fingers when I stopped.

Eventually, Lana finished her magazine and reached her hand out to me. I had assumed she wanted the cat back, but I had grown somewhat attached to it and I shook my head and held the cat to my chest and away from her.

"Katie now Lana no wait give kitty," she said in a warning tone I didn't want to test. She took the cat and smiled at my disheartened pout as I flopped my hand in my lap dramatically.

"See you next week little baby," Lana said as she left the room making my heart skip a beat.

What does she mean little baby? I asked myself for the next five days. It wasn't like I acted like a baby. I didn't even have a baby voice. I was serious and studious and interested in math. I was puzzled and confused and annoyingly turned on remembering Lana's sexy voice and words.

I tided the house like I had the previous week and followed Lana around as she inspected my efforts again.

"Good," she stated as she took out the toy cat and pushed it into my hands. I excitedly cuddled it involuntarily making her laugh and me blush when I had realized what I had done.

"Do Lana's sweet girl like kitty?" She asked patting my bottom over my skirt. I nodded and looked into her grey eyes. Something about them looked different today. Upon closer inspection, she looked different today. Her usual jeans and sweater combination was replaced with a low cut halter dress that came to her knees and heel sandals she had taken off at the door. Her cleavage, usually hidden away showed just how full and round her breasts were and she wore natural-looking makeup making her look sophisticated and mature. Catching me staring at her she laughed.

"What you look like?" Lana said taking my hand and leading me into my bedroom once again. She pushed me on the bed like the previous week and came to sit next to me straight away. She pulled me onto her lap and I sat, my back to her between her thighs as her large breasts pushed into my neck and cheek. She turned my head making me look at her which brought my mouth to her nipple.

"So you like na?" Lana asked pushing her tits into my face. I pulled away from her and caught my breath. I had never been so close to a woman before. In fact, I had never been so close to anybody before. Lana shook her head and pushed my face back between her huge soft jugs and pushed them against my face. They were soft, and smelt like her perfume. I stopped holding onto the toy cat and lifted my hands nervously, wanting to touch her. Sensing my nervousness Lana took each of my hands in hers and placed them on her tits. She showed me how she wanted to be caressed saying, "Like this," as she lifted them up and let the weight fall down. When she took her hands away and let me do it by myself she said, "Yes good. Like this," and closed her eyes making me proud I could please her. She let me play with her for a while before she took my hands and turned me back around so I was facing away from her. She held me in one arm as her other hand reached under my skirt and patted my legs apart.

"Yes good girl," she said as I pushed out my pussy to meet her fingers as she began to run her fingernails over my panties, parting my pussy lips and pulling on them gently.

"Off," Lana stated pulling at my panties. She took her hands away and I wriggled my panties off from under my skirt.

"And this," Lana added pulling my shirt up and over my head. I held the top of my skirt in my hands and looked at her expectantly.

"I didn't said skirt. Do I?" Lana asked making me worried I'd be spanked. I shook my head and turned back around as she pulled me back onto her. She lifted my skirt, grabbing a bunch of it in her hand and stuck her two fingers in my mouth with the other.

"Suck," she commanded sternly. I sucked immediately until she was satisfied, gagging multiple times as she shoved her fingers deeper down my throat saying, "Take it. Take it," over and over in her warning voice. She pulled them out covered in my spit and pushed them straight into my pussy, forcing herself in making me yelp.

"Hush now," she ordered as she roughly fucked my pussy.

"I've never," I said breathlessly, desperate to let her know I was a virgin. She raised an eyebrow and slowed her onslaught enough for me to begin to breath normally again.

"New?" Lana asked as I teared up. She bent her head and kissed my cheek as a tear fell on it.

"New," I replied. In an instant, I saw a gentler, kinder side to her. I guess she no longer saw me like a naughty girl who needed to be fucked into submission. I learned what her replacement was though pretty quick.

"You are baby. My baby. I look for you," Lana said with determination. She stopped fucking my pussy and moved from behind me and jumped off the bed leaving the room. She came back a moment later with her bag. She took out a pacifier and a bib. Sticking the pacifier in my mouth she rubbed my cheek with her thumb looking into my eyes lovingly. She kissed the tip of my nose and put the bib around my neck. She unzipped my skirt and pulled it down quickly. Taking out a pull up with unicorns on it she pulled it over my legs and patted my bottom once it was on.

"Cute," Lana said as she picked up the toy cat and took my hand and led me back to the couch.

"On my lap," she said pulling me to her. She cuddled me close and put the toy cat who I had taken to calling kitty on my chest and began to speak.

"You my baby now," she said as she patted my thigh. I had moments where I felt like an adult in baby gear but I had longer moments where I felt totally at ease dressed in what she had me dressed in. I couldn't understand it. I decided I didn't care and began to play with kitty as she spoke.

"You call me Mommy. No Lana no more understand?" She explained. I nodded again, attempting to take out the pacifier but she put two fingers on it and pushed it back into my mouth.

"Baby do what Mommy says. When baby bad, Mommy spank, when baby good, Mommy love, OK?" She continued. I liked that Lana was being so clear with what was going to happen.

"Baby work sometime Mommy work sometime. Most of time, Mommy will give baby toy and tell her wait for Mommy come back." Lana said. She had clearly thought this through. I spoke through my pacifier, "Mommy. I don't have to work too much, everything I do is passive. I earn money while I sleep." Lana's looked at me confused so I wriggled out of her embrace and walked over to my computer to show her. I sat in her lap and explained to her how my business worked, how I had employees and where she could see the money coming in.

"You are clever baby. I no take your money baby. I just want you. Mommy still work, but maybe not so much," Lana said patting my head.

"Come little girl, Mommy want to watch you play," Lana said putting my laptop on the couch and taking me back to my room.

MDLG Bedtime Stories Book 2

A collection of erotic lesbian age play short stories for ABDL and the Mommy Dommes who love them

By Tina Moore

Mommy To The Rescue

I had loved the woods ever since I could remember. The smell of the pine trees, the soft cool dirt between my toes and the clean air always made me feel so free. Growing up in the city, I had sworn I would move out into the woods the first chance I could and it wasn't more than 6 months ago that the chance finally presented itself. A small wood cabin surrounded by thick bush became available and I had just the right amount of savings to put down the deposit. I packed up all my things, resigned from my job as a stripper and moved into the small country community. I got a new job at the local Bakery and although the pay was a significant cut, I was happy to finally be living a simple country life. The only thing I needed now was a dog. I had decided to buy a big mountain dog, the kind that would keep the wolves away and had contacted a breeder about two hours away. She had a new litter of Russian Bear dogs and I just knew I had to have one.

"Oh she is so sweet, I'll take her," I said to the owner as I picked up the largest chocolate brown female. She had caramel markings around her eyes and on her chest and tail and I was in love. She snuggled into me and after paying the woman and filling out the required paperwork, I took my new little pup home.

"I think I'm going to call you Katya," I said to her as I put her in her travel crate. I climbed into my big black truck and knew that Katya would be riding in the back tray in no time.

"Gosh you are a big girl," I said to her once we reached the cabin and taking her out I let her sniff the air. She barked happily and I watched as she sniffed the boundary of the fence.

"Clever girl, come on," I said opening the door as the first of the winter snow began to fall.

Life progressed calmly and predictably with Katya

going to puppy school and graduating the first in her class. I continued to work at the bakery and had made a few friends with the locals. Everything was going along simply until one afternoon when I took Katya out for a walk. We had gone about 3 miles into the forest when Katya alerted me that something was not right. At first, I thought it was a wolf and took my rifle down from my back and held it ready. I let Katya off her leash but she stayed beside me. I could feel my heart beating hard under my thick winter jacket and stepped heavily making my boots stomp loudly. Katya sniffed the air and before I could tell her to stop she was racing forward into the woods. I began to run after her but stopped when I saw what she had found. She had run about half a mile and by the time I caught up to her, my legs were tired from running through the snow. I panted as I watch Katya sniff the tree and quickly slung my rifle back onto my back. I reached out and touch the half-naked girl Katya had found. She had been tied to a tree with rope that was clearly done up too tight for her as her breaths came out in short but labored moans. Her body was exposed to the harsh snow and wind and looking at her near blue legs, I could tell she had been there for a while.

"Sweetheart, who did this to you," I asked as I took my knife from my belt and cut the ropes off her wrists. I held her up as her legs gave way underneath her and commanded Katya to make sure there was no one else out here. I took my jacket off and wrapped it in her smaller frame as I carried her back to my cabin, followed shortly after by Katya. The girl was clearly older than 18 by the amount of tattoos on her body and she turned in my arms as I carried her back to the cabin and snuggled into my generous breast.

"Warm," she softly said, her voice hoarse from the cold. We got back to the cabin and I was happy I had left the fire burning. Katya went to lay next to it immediately and I placed the girl down on the sofa in front of it while I added logs to it until the flames were high. I made a hot pot of tea and put my things away before bringing the girl a mug of tea. I placed mine down on the coffee table and held the mug to her mouth, helping her to drink. She coughed, and I hoped that the liquid wouldn't hurt her frozen throat. Katya began to sleep, snoring by the fire as I took the girl in my arms and held her against my body, trying to warm her. However innocent my intentions where I was still enjoying having such a beautiful helpless girl in my arms and I pulled my heavy jacket around her firmly.

"My name is Kalista, what's yours?" I asked the girl stroking her hair. She looked up at me and cleared her throat a few times before she spoke.

"I'm Summer," she replied with an angelic voice. Her lips had begun to turn a rosy pink as her body warmed up and her eyes were focused.

"How did I get here? Who are you?" Summer asked as if suddenly realizing she was not tied to a tree anymore.

"My dog Katya found you. You were tied to a tree only wearing your um panties and bra. What happened to you?" I replied. Hearing her name

Katya woke up and came to rest her big head next to Summer's thigh, monstering it in contrast. Summer reached out and patted Katya who craned her neck to meet her touch.

"I was living in the commune, I don't think it is from around here. Where I was, it wasn't snowing. But I tried to escape, the last thing I remember was that I was running through the woods and felt a pinch," Summer said feeling her arm. She turned it around to try and see the back of it and sure enough, there was a needle prick in her flesh.

"Those bastards," Summer said as she began to cry. Seeing her upset, Katya began to lick her hand and I grabbed her by the opening of the jacket and pulled her onto my lap.

"It's OK Summer, you're safe now, we can go to the police and get this all sorted out if you'd like?" I said to her as her little body shook in my arms. I snapped my fingers and Katya went to lay back down by the fire as I stood up and held Summer in my arms.

"Come on baby girl, it's alright," I said as I gently rocked her. She reached up wrapped her arms around my neck and I felt my blue and white flannel soak through as she cried into the nape of my neck. I walked over to where my phone was laying on the kitchen table and dialed 911 and was told to come down to the station right away. Summer didn't want to go but I told her that if anything had happened to her while she was unconscious, the police needed to know. I held her hand while they did the relevant tests and asked her if there was anybody they could ring for her. She shook her head, "I'm an orphan and I never really had any friends. I went to live with the family when I was 18."

"How old are you now?" I asked Summer who had been given baggy clothes from the police. She pushed up the sleeves of the oversized sweater and thought for a moment.

"We didn't celebrate birthdays but I kept a page with all my important dates and I know I'm 22," Summer said trying to remember what she had written in her diary. I told the police she could stay with me to which Summer eagerly agreed and the Police told her they would be in touch if they needed anything else or if they could catch the people who had done this to her.

As we walked back to the truck, Katya stood up in the tray and barked happily to us. Summer reached up and cuddled her before I took her hand and pushed her into the truck. Her clothes were four sizes too big and I looked over at her trying to fold up the jeans around her ankles as I drove out of the station.

"We are going to need to get you some new clothes little one," I said to her making her giggle. It was the first time I had heard her laugh and it warmed my heart. But she made my heart skip a beat when she placed her hand over mine.

"Thanks, Kalista. You're being so nice to me and you don't even know me," Summer almost whispered. I gave her a sideward smirk and winked at her, making her giggle again and I turned my hand over and held hers while I drove us to the store.

"Get whatever you like, you'll need at least five outfits, sweetie," I said taking a shopping trolley and walking her into the store. Summer went quiet and shy and walked behind me, almost hugging my back. I turned around and looked down at her only just realizing that she probably hadn't been in a real store in years.

"It's OK baby, do you really think I'm going to let anything bad happen to you?" I asked her. She just bit her bottom lip and shook her head before I opened my arms and held her until she gently pushed me away and began to look through the store. I stayed by her as she put in jeans, sweaters, and long sleeve shirts. I took her to the shoe department and got her a pair of winter boots for walking in the woods and a pair for going into town. She chose pink cloud pajamas and I bought her three pairs of thigh-high fluffy socks and a selection of bras and panties. I must admit, I liked dressing her, she would twirl in the dressing rooms and playfully pose and I had to remind myself that she wasn't my baby girl.

I have had baby girls before but I hadn't bothered looking for one around here, I had figured that my small little country community was too conservative to be into something like this. But here Summer was, giggling when I pulled on her jeans up and playfully spanked her bottom.

"I've been a good girl, why am I getting spanked?!" Summer giggled. I grabbed her wrist and moved her arms out of my way as I struck her one last time.

"Because I like hearing your giggles little one," I whispered in her ear making her blush. I didn't want her to let me have her just because I had looked after her since Katya found her so I stepped back and let her dress herself.

"If you want to leave, just let me know OK, I'm not about to try and lock you up like they did Summer," I said seriously. Summer turned around and caught me off guard as she wrapped her arms around me and placed her head on my large breasts.

"I know, but you are so nice, you're like a Mommy. I don't want to leave you," she replied making me have to clench my calves so I wouldn't push her down and have my way with her right there on the changing room floor. I thought for a minute and swallowed hard before I spoke again.

"I can be your Mommy if you'd like baby girl," I said softly, hoping that no one else heard. Summer stopped being playful and looked at me very seriously. She took in my larger frame, and full curves, she reached up and ran her hands through my long wavy hair and over my lips.

"OK Mommy," she quietly whispered letting her hands rest on my heavy tits. I had thought it was a good idea to get them done while I was stripping but had felt self-conscious of their huge size before now. Now I had a baby girl who didn't know it yet but would be loving them for hours to come. I smiled and paid for Summer's new clothes before she went back into the changing room to dress herself. When she came out I was impressed with my little baby. She had happily accepted everything that I had told her I wanted her to have and she looked divine.

"My perfect baby," I said as I took her hand and looked at her. She wore pink snow boots with skinny black denim jeans, a white, long sleeve shirt under a white fluffy sweater. She had a black puffer vest and I took her hands and pulled on pink fingerless gloves.

"Come here my little snow bunny," I said cuddling her and running my hands over her body making her giggle and squirm in my arms.

"Summer, I'm home baby girl," I called as I walked into the cabin. It had been two months since I had rescued Summer from the snow and took her in as my little one. We had a good routine of me going to work five days a week, and I had begun to diaper Summer in the evenings. I had told her she was ready to get a job so she didn't get bored during the day and she had been employed at the clothing store we had gone to when I bought her first sets of clothes.

"I'm in here Mommy," Summer said. I hung my bag up on one of the hooks by the door and thought it was strange that Katya wasn't already by my heel. She usually pounced on us when we came home and I looked in front of the fireplace assuming she was there instead. I narrowed my eyes and smiled when I heard Summer's giggles coming from her playroom. I had let one of the rooms of the cabin be for her and although we slept in my bed together, she spent a lot of time in her playroom.

"Look, Mommy, Katy and I are playing hairdressers," Summer said proudly. I looked at what she had done to Katya and laughed. Katy, was obviously not as amused but I was impressed she had let Summer play for as long as they clearly had. Summer had given Katy two big pink bows on both her ears and had put little butterfly clips over her back. Upon seeing me Katy looked in my direction with big sad puppy dog eyes and huffed before licking Summer and putting her head down on the ground as Summer placed more clips in place.

"I think she might have had enough little one, come here and let Mommy get you ready for beddys," I said clapping my hands at Summer and picking her up. She leaned back as I carried her to the bathroom and tried to put clips in my hair.

"Not on Mommy baby girl, Mommy doesn't want to play right now," I told Summer. Summer looked at me confused.

"Why not Mommy?" She asked, stopping like a good girl when I told her no. I sat on the edge of the big bathtub and placed her on my lap before I started running the warm bath water. I lifted Summer's arms up as I took off her shirt and I flicked her nipples until she was forced to pull away from me.

"Because baby girl, Mommy wants to play with you instead," I said rubbing her over her soft cotton shorts. It had been her day off today and she had let the fire burn all day, resulting in a very warm house. I liked it when she did this because she would only wear thigh high socks, short little shorts and a long sleeve tight shirt making me want to ruin her.

I took off her clothes and stuck two fingers into her mouth making her choke while she tried to get them as wet as she could. She had made the mistake of not getting my fingers wet enough before and had not repeated the same mistake since. Taking my fingers out of her mouth I toyed with her asshole making her eyes go wide.

"I think I'm going to fill this pretty little hole tonight baby girl, maybe stretch you until you squeal for me, what do you think?" I said forcing my two fingers into her ass and spreading my fingers apart as far as I could while my other hand began to rub her clit. She moaned and panted shallowly before trying to reply.

"Yes Mommy," Summer moaned making me laugh.

"Yes, Mommy what baby girl, are you just saying yes Mommy because you've forgotten my question? Does doing this make you remember?" I said pushing two fingers into her wet pussy and pushing my other two fingers into her ass making her squeal.

"Yes Mommy, I'll take it and squeal for you," Summer said as I began to roughly fuck her. I could see the water level rising and I edged her until the water was halfway filling the tub. Taking my fingers away from her she moaned in frustration making me laugh as I picked her up and placed her in the tub.

"Get nice and clean for me little one," I said before leaving her to wash herself.

When I came back ten minutes later she was playing with the bath ducks I had bought her.

"Katy is very happy to have stopped playing hairdressers baby girl," I said putting her butterfly clips back in the draw. Summer giggled and splashed water over the tub and onto the floor as she raced two ducks around the bath.

"Come on, up you come," I said placing a towel on my chest and picking her out of the bath. I liked that I was so much bigger than her and that she was unable to fight me. She had tried to resist me a few times, wanting to stay in the water or not wanting to go to bed but between simply picking her up or placing my thigh over her body to pin her down, she was helpless against me.

"Mommy, I don't a diaper tonight, I don't need one," Summer said. She looked at me with a wicked brattiness and I knew that tonight would be fun. I ignored her and took her to my room and threw her down on the bed.

"Did you hear me, Mommy?" Summer said trying to sound authoritative. I laughed.

"Yes I heard you baby girl, I just don't fucking care what you want. I want you in a diaper, so you'll get a diaper. Maybe I might even put two on you for being such a naughty little girl," I said taking off my pants. I watched as Summer watched me undress and I enjoyed putting on a show for her. Music or not, I loved how I moved my body until I was standing over Summer's pretty mouth and lowered my cunt onto her lips.

"Lick it for Mommy," I instructed groping my tits as Summer's tongue dived into my aching hole. I loved smothering her but lifted my thighs letting her breath before lowering myself onto her again. I kept my hand around her neck, feeling her pulse to make sure she could breathe as I forced her to eat my pussy, rocking back and forth and grinding down on her little face.

"You can't get away from Mommy baby girl, stop trying," I said as saw her legs start to wriggle. I lifted off her slightly as she gasped for air, my juices covering her face and neck.

"You'd better make me cum little girl," I said reaching down and slapping her legs apart. I spat on her pussy and rubbed her clit until I felt her moaning into my pussy.

"You're going to cum for Mommy. Say Mommy please baby girl," I commanded, slapping Summer's pussy before finger fucking her again.

"Mommy please," Summer breathlessly moaned, her lips vibrating against my clit making my juices flow again.

"Louder," I said fucking her more roughly, wanting her to be limp with exhaustion.

"Mommy please!" Summer screamed into my cunt as we both came hard at the same time. I liked feeling my cunt squirt into her mouth and felt her tongue lick me clean as I patted her pussy before wetting a black bunny tailed butt plug with her cream.

"Take it, my pretty girl," I said pushing it into her resisting ass. I muffled her cries with my pussy as I filled her only recently deflowered asshole with the toy and stayed on top of her until her cries only came as whimpers.

"Good girl," I said slowly. I got off her and picked her up and cuddled her as I walked into her playroom. I kept cradling her in my arms as I filled her mouth with my nipple and let the weight of my breast fall on her chest and face.

"Suck on Mommy baby girl. I know your pretty ass hurts, but you're being such a good girl for Mommy," I said. Leaving my nipple in her mouth until she had calmed down, I walked over to the cupboard and picked out her outfit. A pink diaper that I had previously cut a hole in the back to fit her little tail for and a baby blue long sleeve shirt. Tonight I'd leave her braless and took out the nipple clamps. I took out a paci gag and leather cuffs and enjoyed the look in her eyes as she saw just how used she was going to be tonight. Holding my breast in both her hands she took my nipple out her mouth.

"Mommy, I," Summer started to say before I pushed my nipple back down her throat.

"I don't remember asking your opinion little one," I said pinching her nose closed and making her gasp around my breast.

"Much better," I said holding her in one arm as my other hand slapped her cheek while she suckled. Growing bored of denying her, I put her down on the floor and began diapering her. She wriggled which just made me shake my head at her and take out a fat vibrating dildo, spitting on it and forcing it up her cunt.

"You're a silly little girl sometimes baby," I said turning it on and fastening her diaper in place. I took the nipple clamps and bit down firmly on her nipples, making them hard as I secured the clamps in place.

"Pretty girl," I said as I watched Summer roll around on the floor in sexual frustration. I knew she wouldn't be cumming for at least an hour and I was going to enjoy every minute of her torture. Next, I put her shirt on and flicked the clamps as I dressed her.

"Please Mommy please," Summer begged as she tried to touch her pussy through her diaper.

"I knew I'd need these," I laughed taking her wrists and cuffing them behind her back. I lifted her up and took her to the living room. I placed her gently down on the sofa and let Katya out for her nightly prowl. Summer moaned loudly on the sofa when I turned the intensity of the vibrator up and I gagged her making her suck on the pacifier as her juices dripped into her diaper.

"Who's my slutty little baby girl," I said coming to sit behind my pretty toy. I moved her so she was sitting between my thighs and I wrapped my legs around hers forcing them apart. Summer grunted in defiance making me laugh and hit her pussy hard over her diaper.

"Give me what I want little baby, you have no choice," I whispered in her ear as I reached around and held her neck while my other hand flicked the clamps up and down. She tried to pull away from me, moaning in tormented frustration before I turned the vibrator onto its highest setting.

"Enjoy my little slut, you can come, you have permission in advance," I said holding her down and watching the flames of the fire. Summer writhed under me, being forced to cum over and over, the flames from the fire making the room hot and Summer began to sweat as she was used. Watching her, I kissed her face and reached into her diaper.

"Mommy is going to finish you off," I said pulling the vibrator from her pussy before slamming it back into her. She turned in my arms and straddled me, pushing the clamps into my breasts which just made her squeal behind the gag.

"There it is," I said as I held her on my lap and fucked her with the thick dildo. Pounding into her pussy, Summer fell limp in my arms before she had even cum and I fucked her defeated body for another hour, filling her hole and feeling her cream squirt out of her used cunt and into her diaper until she shook her head, unable to go on. I smile and gently took the vibrator out of her pussy and undid the gag. She opened her mouth and I pushed the cock into her mouth and she held it there like the good little slut she was. I uncuffed her wrists and she began sucking on the dildo, using both hands like I had trained her too. I smiled and sat against the sofa as I watched her fill her mouth over and over. I let her continue as I took off the clamps, pinching her nipples and pushing the cock down her throat when she flinched.

"I didn't say to stop did I," I said ruffling up the fur of her bunny tail. I could tell she could feel the plug moving inside of her by how wide her eyes became when I moved it. I waited until she had sucked all her pussy juice off the toy before I let her stop and picked her up again.

"Time for bed little one," I said throwing her down and pinning her to the bed with one hand as the other reached into her diaper and pulled the plug out. Summer bit her bottom lip and whimpered as I pulled it from her, making me excited all over again.

"Careful little one, you don't want Mommy to take you again do you?" I said coming to cuddle my beautiful baby girl.

Vote One For Mommy

I've never really been into politics. I mean, don't they all just promise the same thing and under deliver time after time regardless of who gets elected? Anyway, I always had that view, that was until I met Stacey.

Stacey had been the elected Mayor in a small two-bit town for 3 years when I rolled in. I'd moved from the city to get some space after a messy breakup and upon arriving, knew this one-horse town would do the trick. It was quiet, the most exciting thing that happened was local boys who drove tractors during the day, chased girls by the lake at night and played football on the weekends. The girls, well their only real aspiration was to become the wife of whoever the alpha male was of their graduating class, so I knew I'd have no trouble laying low and licking my wounds.

I had been living there for about 3 months before I

ran into her. I was ordering coffee at the one diner in town and saw her out on the street handing people flyers and pinning on badges.

"Looks kinda lame doesn't it?" I heard a voice say behind me. I turned around and there she was. Her beauty had me shook the moment our eyes met. She had that creamy soft type of skin and wave after wave of deep purple hair. Her eyes shone amber as the midday sun shone onto them and her whole presence was like drinking cool ice tea on a hot day. She must have noticed I was lost for words because she sat down and reached over to take my coffee in her hands. I watched as she took a sip, not minding at all drinking from a stranger's cup.

"I'm Stacey, who might you be?" Stacey asked looking at me with a subtle smile.

"Oh, hi, I'm Bianca, but everyone just calls me B," I replied, blushing slightly embarrassed I'd just assumed she'd want to call me B as well. Stacey leaned back and I was mildly aware that people were staring at us but I didn't care. Never in my 24 years had I ever had a conversation with anyone as captivating as Stacey.

"Wow, you've lumped me in the everyone box straight off the bat," Stacey teased only making me more embarrassed. I knew that pleading my case would just create a bigger hole I had obviously already dug myself so I just smiled and looked out the window again. The lady was still there, kissing babies and it made me wonder what kind of moron would let a Politician kiss their baby.

"Weird huh?" Stacey asked interrupting my thoughts. I turned and looked at her blankly after being ripped out of my thoughts. She tilted her head to the woman outside.

"I never kiss babies, in fact, I have a completely different pre-election game plan. Hers is weak," Stacey explained. I looked at her with her mid 30's youth and outlandish hair color and looked back out to the woman on the street.

"You mean, you are running against her?" I asked, unsure of what she was trying to say. My confusion made Stacey laugh and she nodded.

"I'm the Mayor around here. Didn't you know?" Stacey asked helping me to finally understand why people were looking at us. They weren't looking at me so much as looking at her.

"Politician huh," I said not being quite sure where to place this new information.

"So, your game plan is to drink newcomer's coffee and rip shreds off the opposition?" I teased. Stacey laughed and I caught myself having that awful feeling. The one that latches onto your heart and races through your body, the feeling that only leads to heartbreak.

"No, this is actually me trying to flirt with you. But clearly, it's not working. Let me try again, would you like to come to dinner Friday night?" Stacey asked. I couldn't believe the nerve of this woman. I sat back in the booth and looked her up and down. I didn't like how much power she had over me.

"I'm busy sorry," I said getting up and leaving the bill on the table with a generous tip.

For a family owned joint, they did a great job.

"What are you being so busy with?" Stacey asked. I really wasn't expecting her to keep trying, hell if someone had shut me down the way I was her, I'd of wanted to disappear and never been seen again. I looked at her and tried to study her face. What is it about this one? I thought to myself. A waitress dropped a tray of forks startling me out of my trance and I quickly wrote down my number on a napkin.

"Here, give me a call and we can arrange something," I said sliding her the napkin with my name and number before I pulled my coat on and walked out the door. I didn't need to turn around to know her eyes were on me, I could feel them. Her stare had been playful and mischievous like she knew I'd give in to her, but there was something else. A daring, a challenge, she looked at me as though she knew my deepest secrets and was waiting for me to discover them too.

A week passed and I hadn't heard from Stacey. It

hurt the first few days, but I just filed it under, typical female bullshit, and got on with the rest of the week. I'd found a job at the local library and enjoyed being to hide all day in the shelves and books. The only other person who worked there was an older lady who had probably only hired me so she had someone to talk to. I didn't mind though and our hour-long conversations over tea and cake made me forget for a moment what I had left behind. She told me about the history of this town, who the true owners of this land were and who the key players were. Like all small towns, the "founding families" thought they were more important than everyone else and owned most of the commercial real estate.

"What about Stacey?" I asked her during one of our cake and tea breaks. She smiled behind her cup and it made me wonder what kind of evil this old woman had seen.

"Why do you ask about her?" She replied. I was aware she had answered my question with a question and knew that whatever she told me would have multiple meanings.

"I think you know by that look on your face," I bluntly replied. She put her teacup on the saucer and looked at me, almost as if she was trying to read my mind.

"Be careful with her, she is a powerful woman and will stop at nothing to get what she wants," the woman replied matching my seriousness. She got up and began putting the books back away, signaling that it was the end of our conversation.

I had all but given up on Stacey when my phone rang one lazy Saturday morning.

"Oh, I haven't interrupted something important have I?" Stacey asked. I could tell by the fake concern in her voice my response would not shift her desire so I lied in my reply.

"No, I was just doing some housework," I said then held my breath. She was the sort of person you desperately wanted to be liked by and I could feel myself getting sucked into her trap.

"Well then, how about after you finish, we go for a walk around the lake. It's beautiful this time of year," Stacey replied before quickly adding, "I'll see you in two hours by the south side dock," before hanging up. I knew she was bad news. I could feel it in my blood but there I was, two hours later waiting for her. She reminded me of the woman I had spent months hiding from, the one who had taken me in and created a safe space for me just to turn that space into a nightmare. I knew the look Stacey had in her eyes, I'd seen it before, but I just couldn't seem to shake it. I decided it was best to stay away from her and I turned around to go back to my car but saw her walking towards me. Damn, I thought to myself.

"Hi there," Stacey said pulling me into her and kissing me on the cheek.

"Aren't you just the cutest," she said holding my hand and taking a long look at me. I wasn't wearing anything particularly special, just some baggy jeans and a t-shirt, my hair in a ponytail and a navy cap. I had decided it was warm enough to wear my new orange flip flops so my toes where freshly pedicured. I guess I did look good, but she looked at me as though she was about to devour me, our opinions didn't match.

"Thanks," I said as she took my arm in hers and began slowing walking around the lake.

"Who hurt you, baby," Stacey suddenly said breaking the silence and making me pull away from her, my guard going up instantly. I looked at Stacey full of rage.

"What the fuck is your game?" I said almost growling at her. Stacey's gaze softened from its usual playful challenge and she slowly reached for my hand.

"I can tell I'm not the first person to call you baby, B," Stacey said tenderly.

"First of all, you don't know shit and secondly, I'm out," I said turning and leaving her standing alone.

I was almost back at my car when I heard her running after me. I had half a mind to just ignore her and drive away but something made me stay. I turned around and saw her doubled over and panting.

"Just...wait," Stacey panted. I waited but I also watched. I watched how to had to take deep breathes to regain her composure, I watched how she had to pace up and down with her hands on her head to get her breathing under control but I watched how she changed from her usual arrogant demeanor to something kind and soft.

"Why do I excite you?" I asked just before she was about to speak. Stacey closed her mouth and looked at me and I could tell she was tossing up giving me an honest answer or not.

"Honestly, you look like prey and I'm guessing that's what excites most people. Maybe even the one who hurt you. But I see more than that and I don't want to hurt the small spaces of you," Stacey said and I was happy she was honest. I looked down and thought about how to reply.

"So you want to love me, take me home and make me yours?" I said plainly.

"Something like that," Stacey replied taking

a step closer towards me.

"Don't," I said making her stop.

"Gosh, you're just like a little pound pup all angry and snappy," Stacey said.

"Yeah, so back off and give me time," I replied, happy to see her nod her head and take a step back. We stayed like that, just looking at each other and resting in each other's energy.

"You wanna tell Mommy what happened baby?" Stacey said as the sunset. She had come to rest on the side of my car and had stood beside me watching the sun dip behind the mountain range.

"Not really," I said resting my head on her shoulder. She reached up and stroked my cheek affectionately and didn't seem to mind me flinching under her touch.

"I'm not going to hurt you, sweetheart," Stacey said standing up and turning to face me.

"That's what she said too," I replied. Stacey waited for me to speak again and when I didn't she reached her hands into her pockets and rocked back and forth on her boot heel.

"Aren't you cold?" Stacey said shivering. I hadn't noticed the weather change until then.

"But I don't want to leave," I replied giving her a chance.

"Then let's not, but could we go somewhere warm?" She asked. I liked that she asked me instead of just planning it. I nodded and unlocked my car but she waited until I smiled at her and she got in.

"Where are you taking me, baby?" Stacey asked reaching for my hair to stroke. I didn't flinch this time, I smiled and moved my head to find her hand.

"Mine," was all I said in reply. I drove in silence and Stacey seemed to think that was her cue for sharing her expertise with me.

"I've done this a couple of times before. I really like having a baby to look after and I knew you were a little girl the minute I saw you. I couldn't figure you out though like usually babies don't make me wait to love them, usually, it's me pushing them away because they get too attached too quickly," Stacey said as I took the long way home. Not because I didn't want her in my space, but because I was enjoying her rambling and found her voice sexy.

"But you, you put me on ice straight outta the gate and I figured someone like you ending up in a town like this wasn't for any good reason and when you were flinching before...I'm sorry someone hurt you," Stacey continued. I pulled into my driveway and turned to her, turning the car off.

"It wasn't just someone. It was a list of someone's because I let them. I'm trying to break that pattern. So, don't be like them, because I'm not trying to recreate my past anymore," I stated. Stacey nodded and followed me inside.

"I hope you know nothing is going to happen tonight Stacey," I said leading her through the house, giving her a quick tour.

"I know that. I honestly don't think anything will happen for a long while yet, but that's just fine with me," Stacey said. I couldn't believe how different she was to the absolute hurricane I had first met. Here she was calm, patient, and almost soothing.

"Here," I said passing her a beer and clinking the top of hers with mine. She smiled and drank deeply before looking at me.

"So, I grew up here, but my family comes from upstate. They moved here when I was 3 so this town is all I know. I've gone overseas on holidays but I always come back, it's got that magical feel to it," Stacey said giving me the knowledge I didn't ask for. She looked at me and I took a deep breath knowing it was my turn now.

"I grew up on the east coast, I'm not telling you where, and I moved here to escape a person who used being a 'Domme' as a cover up for being simply, abusive," I replied taking another sip of my drink. I could tell she wanted more and decided I'd allow her to have her answers I continued.

"She took punishments way too far for me, isolated me from my friends and said awful things about my family. She didn't listen to my concerns and didn't respect my limits and tried to dominate the things I didn't submit to her. She wasn't like that at the beginning so I stayed with her thinking that she'd go back to who she was when we first got together and it took me way too long to realize that she was never kind or caring or loving, that it was just her way to lure me in," I replied. Stacey had finished her beer by the time I had finished telling her my story and she listened fully, making me nervous to have someone so present.

"That's definitely worth hiding from," Stacey replied. I like that she didn't try to touch me. I looked at her and she smiled at me making my heart flutter.

"And there you were, with all your bravado and confidence do you see why I ran from you?" I asked making Stacey laugh.

"Bravado?" She questioned nodding her head accepting my judgment.

"Well, bravado aside, I've liked this. We should do it again sometime," Stacey said getting up and heading to the door, not wanting to outstay her welcome. She reached for the door handle and our hands touched as my hand found it's placed on top of hers making her turn to me.

"Don't," I said this time making her unsure of what I was meaning. Stacey didn't seem to mind as I took her hand and led her to my room.

"B, I," Stacey started to say but was cut off by my kiss. I liked that she tried to push me back before she got lost in my kiss and reached around to hold me close to her. Her breath was hot on my neck as she held my head and kissed down my body.

"You are beautiful," she whispered stopping herself as she grabbed the top of my jeans pulling a fist of denim passionately wanting to be let in but accepting when I shook my head no.

"Feel this," Stacey said taking my hand and placing my fingers on her pulse.

"I'm racing," she added making me pull away slowly and look at her.

"You stopped," I said happily making her confused.

"Of course I did," Stacey replied as if it was

the only option in the world.

"You asked me to, remember?" She said making me laugh.

"Yeah, I'm just happy you did," I said sitting on my bed.

"I'm not a rapist, only rapists don't stop. You can't call them anything but that if they don't stop when you ask them too little one," Stacey said laying down next to me. She pulled me close and I snuggled into her, noticing her sweet perfume for the first time. I buried my face between her warm breasts and let her stroke my hair as she slowly rocked me.

"I know you're going to be guarded for a long while yet baby girl, but Mommy is here now and I'll wait for you, always," Stacey said lovingly. I giggled and pulled away to look up at her.

"That should be your campaign slogan, you could be like, vote one for Mommy," I playfully said resulting in hearing Stacey's hearty laugh and feeling her tickle my tummy.

Baby Girls Get Sippy Cups

"Last drinks," came the routine call from Lacie, the bar owner of the 67th. The 67th was the only bar for miles on a strip of dirt that called itself a road, in the middle of two towns. The 67th had been in Lacie's family for generations and anyone in 100 miles could tell you about their own story of the 67th.

"To the big fella," someone yelled and the local crowd raised their glasses to the photo of Lacie's Dad which hung over the beer taps. This always happened after last drinks was called and she had grown to love the way her Father was remembered. Closing the bar, Lacie walked out to the carpark and smiled up to the stars. Her Father had been gone for five years now but every night it felt like he was still there, shining in the bright stars over the desert dunes and wiping their faces with sand like he used to with the bar towels. He was always so playful like that, Lacie thought as she sat on her motorbike.

"See you all tomorrow," Lacie said to a group of men still talking out the front as she revved her bike, driving off into the early morning sun as before she could hear their replies.

Lacie tiredly walked into the tattoo parlor a few hours later and fell asleep while her right half sleeve was finished.

"Only Lacie could fall asleep while getting ink done," the artist said laughing as she worked. She left Lacie in the seat for the next 5 hours knowing she would be working again that night.

"Whoa, guys you should have woken me up, sorry," Lacie said sleepily waking up as a customer came in making the bell chime.

"You're right, don't even worry about it," the artist who did Lacie's sleeve replied receiving a large tip. She looked at Lacie questioningly.

"It's sleep money," Lacie said laughing before she walked out and got on her bike. She drove to the bar, she knew she didn't have to work for a few hours but didn't mind going in early, it hardly felt like work. It was more, how she spent her life. She liked the local guys and their stupid traditions, ongoing pool and darts competitions and jokes. She liked watching the newly legal kids rock up and try to fit in, nervous to be there or overconfident to try and hide their nerves. She liked watching lovers and fly throws, the people that needed a drink and people that used it as medicine. She liked it all and yet, it felt hollow. It didn't matter how those nights were filled, who she gave free drinks too, who she made sure got home safe or who she threw out, when the lights got turned off and the sun came up, it was like she had been in a dream.

Lacie restocked the bar and waited for her 7 pm regulars, setting up their snacks in their spots knowingly. She had turned around to pour herself a shot of tequila and choked on it as she turned back to see a blonde hair girl with brown eyes staring back at her.

"Jesus girl," Lacie coughing and hitting her own chest to push the alcohol down. The girl looked down and giggled making Lacie smirk back once she had stopped coughing.

"I'm going to need some ID sweet thing," Lacie said shaking her head, disbelief that this girl could be a minute older than 21. The girl rolled her eyes just adding to Lacie's amusement and slid her ID over the bar.

"Some face you've got there," Lacie said quickly calculating the girl's 26 years of age.

"Yeah, I get that a lot," the girl replied. Lacie leaned back against the shelf of spirits and slung the bar towel over her shoulder.

"What'll it be then?" Lacie asked. She saw a couple of regulars make their way in and was happy they knew better than to interrupt her.

"What am I allowed?" The girl replied making Lacie bite her bottom lip and raise an eyebrow.

"It'll be cocktails all night then, think you can handle that?" Lacie replied. The girl took out a black Amex and flicked it across the bar.

"Can you?" The girl said making Lacie laugh as she began making the girl's first drink.

As the night progressed Lacie made it very clear who her priority was and was happy most people respected that. The locals ordered but didn't make a point of overstaying their welcome at the bar and Lacie was happy the sweet girl she was happily getting drunk turned down the people who asked her to dance.

"Are you turning them down because you can't dance or are you worried I'll kick your drunk ass out when you try to stand and fall back down again?" Lacie teased making the girl take a piece of ice and throw it at her.

"My my baby girl, you are naughty," Lacie said taking the girl's chin in her hand and making her head shake. Lacie watched as the girl's drunk eyes settled back before she pushed her hair back affectionately.

"I reckon you're done after that one sweetpea," Lacie said handing the girl, who she had learned was called Cleo, her card back. She never had any intention of charging for this night. Unknowingly, Cleo smiled and put the card back into the top pocket of her denim overalls and happily accepted the water Lacie replaced her unfinished cocktail with.

"This had been fun," Cleo said as she stumbled getting up.

"But I really need to go," she added. Lacie nodded knowingly.

"Yeah, I was wondering how long you'd last. The bathroom is just behind that wall there," Lacie said pointing around to the corner making Cleo laugh.

"No I mean I need to go home," Cleo said making Lacie wonder how she could hold all those drinks.

"I can't let you drive home sweetie," Lacie said snapping her fingers to a guy at the booth who stood up and came to the bar.

"Lock it up for me, I'm taking her home," Lacie said and the guy, her cousin, nodded and began to get to work.

"You don't have to, I can just catch a taxi," Cleo said holding onto Lacie as she led her out of the bar.

"Doubt it, there's no taxi's at this hour baby," Lacie said going to her bike.

"Here," she said helping Cleo on. She felt Cleo's body resting on her as she slowly drove off and reached her strong arms around Cleo's body pulling her close as she turned into the street address Cleo had given her.

"Nice digs," Lacie said turning the bike off and helping Cleo off.

"Thanks," Cleo sleepily said.

"You can't come in," Cleo said nervously, suddenly very awake.

"Alright, I won't," Lacie said laughing, wondering why Cleo was so nervous.

"It's not that I don't want you to it is just that. Um, I, my house is messy," Cleo said, obviously trying to find any reason as to not allow Lacie in.

"What do think I would do? Just barge in and set up camp?" Lacie said kissing Cleo on her forehead.

"I'm glad you're home safe, bring your cute self back to mine some time," Lacie said turning on her heel and heading back to her bike. Cleo stayed standing by the front door as she watched Lacie drive off into the night before she quickly opened her door and felt her diaper become wet under her overalls.

Lacie hadn't seen Cleo for a couple of weeks and had all but given up having a second chance with her when Cleo was suddenly sitting in front of her one quiet night.

"Jesus, will you stop doing that," Lacie said, once again chocking on her drink.

"I am just sitting here, you're the one who obviously is not aware of what's going on around you," Cleo said cheekily.

"Is that so," Lacie replied. Cleo smiled and pointed to the premixed drinks in the fridge.

"No cocktails tonight?" Lacie laughed as she passed Cleo a pink bottle of premixed vodka and raspberry flavoring.

"No, definitely not!" Cleo exclaimed sipping her drink and looking at Lacie.

"I felt it you know," Lacie said taking a gamble. The night she had ridden Cleo home, she had felt the softness of her diaper when she had turned into the corners and held Cleo close. Knowing she was right in her guess by Cleo's fearful eyes and stunned silence, Lacie smiled.

"You don't have to be worried, I think it's cute," Lacie said making Cleo breath again but look around nervously.

"As if I'd out you little girl," Lacie said placing her hand on top of Cleo's, happy when she didn't pull away.

"Is that why you didn't want me to come in?" Lacie near whispered. Cleo nodded her head and looked down.

"I kinda don't really know what I'm doing with it, I'm sorta new," Cleo whispered back.

"I don't think there's a right or wrong way baby, there's just your way," Lacie said tenderly making Cleo smile and sit back.

"So, what now?" Cleo said wondering what all this meant.

"Hold that thought," Lacie said as she spent the next 20minutes serving an out of town football team who seemed to make it their nights mission to drink the bar dry.
When Lacie turned back to where Cleo had been sitting, she saw an empty chair. Rushing out from behind the bar, she ran out to see Cleo leaning on her bike.

"Baby," Lacie said involuntarily, relieved Cleo wasn't gone.

"Want to go?" Lacie asked as she walked over to Cleo who was nodding her head.

"Can I come in this time?" Lacie asked buckling a helmet under Cleo's chin.

"Maybe," Cleo replied cheekily, giving Lacie the feeling that a maybe was going to turn very quickly into a yes. Lacie knew she didn't have to drive slow and this time raced through town enjoying Cleo's giggles in her ear as she rested her head on her shoulder. Arriving at Cleo's home in no time at all, Lacie took her helmet off and walked her to the door.

"Well goodnight," Lacie said pulling Cleo into her for a hug. She took her time before she let Cleo go, slowly but very purposely running her fingers through her long blonde hair, grabbing a fist full and pushing her face into her chest as her other hand grabbed her ass and squeezed making Cleo gasp and push her pussy onto Lacie's thigh.

"Don't stop," breathed Cleo as she reached for her keys in her jeans pocket and tried to open the door.

"I was hoping you'd say that," Lacie said as she dipped her head and brought Cleo's mouth up to hers, kissing her passionately as the door opened behind them making them fall into the house. Lacie kicked the door shut once they were both inside and pushed Cleo onto the floor as she began to ravish her body. Letting her body fall onto Cleo's, Lacie used her knee to nudge Cleo's thighs apart and flexed her quad against Cleo's pussy making her moan. Lacie kissed down her neck and held Cleo's head gently in her arms as she began to rhythmically pound her thigh against Cleo's pussy, making her gasp each time she was thumped. Cleo reached down to unbutton her jeans, wanting the release to come faster. But Lacie took her hand and held her wrist down, looking into her eyes.

"Alright?" Lacie asked, hoping Cleo was happy to submit this to her. Cleo nodded as she was pounded by Lacie's muscular thigh, grinding down on it and feeling her clit be teased edging her and keeping her there, frustrating her beyond belief.

"Are you going to be Mommy's good girl tonight baby," Lacie whispered in Cleo's ear as she just moaned in response, rolling her head back and closing her eyes.

"Ask Mommy if you want to cum baby," Lacie said as she felt Cleo grab at her full tits as she shuddered and tried to fight her own orgasm.

"Please Mommy," Cleo desperately begged breathlessly, a low moan escaping as Lacie whispered, "Yes," in her ear as she moved her arm from around Cleo's head and gently rested her hand on her neck, not sure how much she liked or if this was OK at all. Cleo grabbed her hand and pressed it firmly down on her neck and Lacie smiled as she took the hint and squeezed tightly, making Cleo's eyes open widely as she came. Swallowing hard and trying to lift her hips under Lacie's body wanting a quicker release Cleo groaned in frustration as she was forced to come slowly. Lacie smiled in satisfaction as she kissed Cleo passionately, enjoying feeling Cleo's breath coming in short shallow gasps.

"Show Mommy Cleo," Lacie said unbuttoning Cleo's jeans and letting her finally take them off. Cleo reached down and practically ripped them off her but froze when she realized that Lacie could now see her diaper. Lacie kissed Cleo loving on her cheek as she placed her hand on the front of Cleo's diaper and rubbed her slowly.

"Don't be nervous. You look cute," Lacie said looking down at Cleo's worried face. She turned her head and looked away. Lacie got off her and sat back as Cleo rested on her elbows.

"I really liked that, but I am kinda exhausted now Mommy," Cleo said, hesitantly saying, mommy. Lacie scooted over to where she was resting and held her in her arms.

"Then tell me what you need now," Lacie said making Cleo melt into her arms.

"You mean you don't want to go?" Cleo asked looking up at Lacie who shook her head no.

"I want to stay, if you'll let me," Lacie replied. Cleo rolled her body into Lacie's who held her for a long time. As her ass became numb from sitting on the floor for so long, Cleo stood up and reached for Lacie's hand.

"Shower?" Cleo asked. Lacie followed Cleo to the bathroom.

"I like calling you Mommy," Cleo nervously said, hoping Lacie liked it too.

"That's nice since that's my name," Lacie said. Cleo started to take off her clothes but was stopped by Lacie.

"Let me," she said lifting Cleo's shirt over her head. Cleo giggled as Lacie ran her fingernails over her body giving her goosebumps. Lacie took off Cleo's diaper and watched as she got into the shower and began to wash herself.

"You really are a beautiful baby girl," Lacie said almost in a trance looking at Cleo. It made her smile and she drew a smiley face on the glass shower screen as the room began to get hot and steamy.

"I'm not sure what to do next," Cleo said to Lacie.

"What do you mean?" Lacie replied taking off her clothes and joining Cleo in the shower.

"Well, do we keep going with the baby stuff or do you wanna stay the night? Like, what do we do?" Cleo explained. Lacie used Cleo's body wash as she thought about what to do next.

"What space do you feel like you are in?"

Lacie asked making Cleo think for a second.

"A big girl one," Cleo replied moving so Lacie could rinse off.

"Do you want to stay there? Or do you want to be Mommy's good little girl?" Lacie asked as the water flowed over her athletic body making her skin glisten.

"Mommy's good girl," Cleo said shifting her feet nervously hoping Lacie would be down for it.

"Good," Lacie replied, making Cleo give a sideward smile.

"Let me dry you off before you go to get what you want me to dress you in tonight. Make sure you bring me a diaper, I don't want my little girl going to bed without one," Lacie said making Cleo's mouth gape open with just how Mommy like Lacie suddenly sounded.

"Oh baby, does it sound just like you always hoped it would?" Lacie questioned making Cleo just nod her head as Lacie dried her and gently slapped her ass as she left the bathroom to follow the instructions Lacie had given.

Cleo waited patiently in her room for Lacie who appeared 5minutes later. She was just wearing a towel wrapped around her waist, her abs and strong arms made Cleo blush. Lacie didn't say anything as she went to Cleo's cupboard and put on one of her t-shirts and a pair of short pajama shorts.

"Now, what does the baby have for Mommy?" Lacie asked, turning to face Cleo. Cleo held up what she had picked and giggled with Lacie jumped on her bed.

"Then lay down so I can get you ready little one," Lacie said as Cleo obediently laid on her back.

"What a good girl," Lacie tenderly said as Cleo stayed still while Lacie diapered her. It was the first time Lacie had done anything like this and was impressed with herself how naturally it came. She took the colorful dino onesie and gently dressed Cleo.

"There, Mommy's little princess is almost ready for bed. Have you forgotten something though baby?" Lacie asked. Cleo looked around her room and wondered what Lacie could mean.

"Here, open wide little girl," Lacie said taking a fistful of Cleo's hair and pulling her head back. Cleo gasped and Lacie took the opportunity to put her pacifier in her mouth before letting her hair go.

"Now you are ready for bed little girl," Lacie said snuggling into bed with Cleo. Cleo pushed her face into the side of Lacie's full breast happily snuggling into it.

"Next time you come into the bar, you'll get your drink in a sippy cup, little miss, baby girls get sippy cups," was the last thing Cleo heard before she fell asleep.

High School Reunion

I had done the usual things after High School, got a part-time job, went to University, graduated and now worked in the profession I had studied for. I enjoyed holidaying with friends or traveling alone, nothing overly extraordinary but still what I would consider a nice life.

It had been ten years since I had graduated from High School and I could feel the reunion vibes a month before I got my letter in the mail. High School, gross, I thought to myself as I opened the envelope. I was the loser in High School, the one which even the other bully victims didn't want to hang out with. I had overheard a popular girl once say she couldn't decide if she'd go to this party or that one and I remember wondering what it must feel like to be invited to so many parties you could choose which one you wanted to attend. I'd never been invited to a party and I had a sneaky suspicion the only reason I'd been invited to the reunion was an emailing glitch.

As the evening of the reunion approached, I was still unsure if I should go or not. I couldn't help but wonder how everyone had turned out. I wondered if the popular girls were still the beautiful ones or if my career as a makeup artist had given me the lifestyle that surpassed theirs. Ten years ago I would not have believed anyone if they had told me where I would be today. Back then I was the orphaned daughter of a crack-addicted Mother who didn't know who my Father was, living in foster care with 5 other kids and wondering where my next meal would come from. I had taken all the pain of being freezing in the winter because my clothes weren't warm enough and falling in love with my gym teacher because she was the only person who had ever shown me kindness and turned my life into something little girls dream about. I had gone to Paris and Milan for fashion week for the last 5 years, met the most incredible people I could call my friends and never had to worry about staying warm or having enough food. I still shied away from romance and had only had a handful of romantic encounters, and if I'm honest, those people looked like my high school gym teacher.

She would always wear these mid-thigh black shorts and some type of colored t-shirt with sneakers that matched. Her hair was always out and only when she'd get really into a game would she put it up, flexing her big muscular arms as she did so. She'd caught me staring at her a number of times but she always just smiled and didn't embarrass me about getting caught. When the other girls had excluded me in a game she'd change the game so that there were no teams and although I knew she was just being a good teacher, I loved her kindness. She had a deep laugh and a serious, stern voice that even made the boys taken her seriously.

I shook my head, trying to stop thinking about her and put the reunion letter down. I still had four days to think about going or not and I had to get to work.

Four days came faster than I had thought and although I'd RSVP'ed I was going, I still was unsure. What if it is just like high school all over again? What if they laugh at me? Wait, laugh at me for what? Driving a Lambo? Holidaying in the Caribbean? They've got nothing on me now, I thought, checking myself. My makeup was, obviously, flawless and I had bought a black backless dress for the occasion. Teamed with strappy metallic silver heels and a silver clutch, I looked wonderful. However, I couldn't stop the slight tightening of my stomach as nerves raced through my body. Wishing I could take a shot of tequila before I drove, I put the bottle down and made my way to the party.

This was a huge fucking mistake, I said to myself as I walked up to the long path that led up to the school. I had to park down the bottom of the hill and although my heels were comfortable, I felt shaky on them. I passed the tennis courts where I use to play tennis and the memory of the popular girls deliberately hitting me with the ball came into my mind. Forget that, it's over now, they can't hurt you anymore, I thought as I approached the entrance to a building which was clearly where I was meant to be going. There was a woman standing out the front with a table set up and balloons tied to the ends.

"Name?" The woman said in a bubbly voice. Before I could say my name she was already gasping and holding her hand to her chest.

"Hayley? Hayley Swanston?" She asked. I looked at her and couldn't remember her name to save myself.

"Yes?" I replied, wishing she would tell me her name. Seeing that I had forgotten, she rolled her eyes.

"Sophie McBridge! We use to play tennis together!" The woman replied joyfully. I remember what Sophie McBridge used to look like and this woman standing in front of me was a far cry from any of my memories. The Sophie that I remember was slender and athletic, this woman was a solid three past Sophie's wide with eyes that were sunken in.

"Oh Sophie, right sorry, gosh it's been such a long time," I replied, unsure of what to say. Sophie just nodded her head and handed me my name sticker. I looked at it and looked back at her and she took it from my hands and placed it just above my right breast, rubbing it down.

"There, you're ready to go, top floor, the view is fantastic," Sophie said knowingly and I just smiled as I walked inside and found the elevator. Holy shit, Sophie McBridge, I thought as the elevator made its long ascent.

Reaching the top, the doors slid open and a party in full swing greeted me. It was a lot to take in all at once. There was music playing and people mingling and I really just wanted to turn and run away but as I was about to, I saw on the projected wall display of photos from my tennis days. I walked over to the wall and stared at the girl who stared plainly back at me. With eyes that begged for love, anyone's love I looked at that girl and wished I could have told her then what I know now.

"Wow, Hayley?" A high pitched voice cut through the masses of conversations and music making me really want to run away. I forced myself to turn and look at the tall slender blonde behind me. She had always been beautiful, with her angular face and full pink lips, it was no wonder she had been the most popular girl in high school.

"Hi Allison," I heard myself say, annoyed at the slight yearning in my voice for her approval. She looked me up and down and stepped forward, embracing me as though she hadn't spent the better part of our high school years together making my life a living hell. I held my breath during the embraced but gasped when she pinched my waist with both her hands.

"Not the little chubbsie anymore," she said

grabbing at me making the women who had begun to form around her laugh.

"Remember what we use to call you, little piggy," Allison said making the woman laugh even harder. I looked at them and for the first time, I saw them for who they truly were. Ugly, they were plain, old fashioned ugly with a deprivation to try and make others feel ugly to hide the fact that they were awful human beings. I smiled, reclaiming my power and looked Allison dead in the eye.

"No I don't remember, I am too busy driving my Lambo and being gifted tickets to events you could never pay for to worry about what some stupid, ugly, never gonna come up bitches like you said ten years ago," I said quickly turning away and walking in the opposite direction trying to get away from them as fast as I could.

I made my way to the long table of drinks which had been set up by the wall-length window overlooking a sports field. Gosh, cool set up, I thought seeing how the school had changed. They had somehow managed to get a grass field on top of one of the other buildings and I suppose during sporting events this room would be the one to host the VIP's. I was deep in my thoughts when I heard a familiar voice behind me, "Someone learned how to handle herself." I swallowed hard, I knew who this was. Turning around, my beer in my hand, I locked eyes on her. My beautiful gym teacher and her beautiful face.

"Hi, um Ms," I started to say stopping when I saw her shake her head.

"You can call me Veronica now Hayley," Veronica said making me blush, apparently to her amusement.

"I see not everything has changed," Veronica said making me laugh and wish like mad I could stop going red.

"Are you still teaching?" I asked trying to steer the conversation away from me. Veronica moved her hand behind my back to grab a drink, making me move forward to get out of her way but only resulting in closing the gap between us, making me blush harder. I was grateful she didn't seem to mind.

"Yeah, apparently gym class is my calling. What about you? Where have you ended up?" Veronica asked taking a sip from her drink and motioning that I should follow her outside. The air was cooler on the sporting field and I liked that there weren't so many people out here.

"I'm a makeup artist," I replied once we had found our spot. I liked seeing that I took Veronica by surprise.

"A makeup artist?" She asked choking on her drink.

"Is that so hard to believe?" I questioned. I didn't want her to think I was lying.

"No, it's just, that's a pretty brutal industry, I would have thought you'd want something a little, gentler after everything," Veronica explained. I leaned against a wall and sighed.

"Apparently pain is my calling," I said dramatically making her laugh.

"No honestly, it's a really good job and I

really love it. This place taught me all I needed to know about how to deal with bitches and life taught me the rest," I said honestly. Veronica raised an eyebrow and looked impressed.

"Well, cheers to you then little miss," she said making my heart skip a beat. She must have sensed it because she bit her bottom lip and looked me up and down.

"Don't," I said quietly pushing her away.

"You're hardly my student anymore, I haven't seen you for ten years. I can look at all of you now if I want to," Veronica said making my stomach turn.

"I saw the way you use to. I bet you thought about me when you were all alone at night in your room. I bet you still do," she added taking a step closer and wrapping an arm around my waist. My legs almost buckled as I felt her muscled arm flex against me as she pulled me closer to her. I don't know if it was the alcohol or if seeing her again just blinded my consciousness but when her lips met mine I opened my mouth instinctively. I reached up and wrapped my arms around her neck, standing on my tippy toes and moaned in her mouth feeling her hand on the back of my head pushing my mouth deeper into hers. I lost grip of my beer bottle and it fell to the grass as I let the fire of this kiss ravage through my being. Stopping, I pulled away to see that some people had been watching us and I turned to leave only to feel Veronica grab my wrist.

"Wrong way sweetheart, my car is over there," she said in her sexy authoritarian manner. I smiled at her and eagerly took the hand she offered for me to hold as she led me down the hill of the sports field to the staff carpark.

The staff carpark hadn't changed one bit and I giggled to myself making Veronica look at me playfully.

"I use to walk this way to first period, the long way, just to see if your car was here because I wanted to know if you were here," I said as we walked through the carpark.

"I know. I use to be able to see you search

the number plates until you found mine and smile to yourself when you did from my office, it used to be over there remember?" Veronica said lovingly.

"How come you never tried to find me after I graduated?" I asked, aware of just how little I sounded.

"Because I'm not perverted and you were still a kid even though you thought you were so big and grown up graduating high school," Veronica said affectionately.

"Anyway, I've got you now haven't I?" Veronica said opening her car door and buckling me in. I looked down at her large hands running over my seat belt and I hoped that she'd want me for longer than just this night.

"Yeah, you do," I said awestruck as Veronica stood up and went to the driver's side. I wish I could have felt less taken by her but as she placed her hand on my thigh and lifted my dress up slowly I couldn't help but let her have her fun. When we stopped at a red light, she leaned over and kissed me making my heart flutter like a school girl and I was grateful I was sitting because my legs would have given way I'm sure. A car behind us beeped their horn making Veronica break the kiss and laugh as she began driving again.

"You are such a sweet girl in your grown-up dress and pretty heels Hayley," Veronica said slowing the car down, as we began to drive into a leafy neighborhood. I didn't really know why she was speaking like this, but I liked it. It made me feel protected and safe with her muscular body and dominating presence, being soft and loving just to me.
She stopped the car and snapped her fingers at me when I tried to get out of the car.

"Let me baby girl," Veronica said making my pussy tingle. I had never had someone display such affection to me before and it was blowing my mind. I held my breath as she unbuckled my seat belt and looked me in the eye.

"Little girls need their Mommy to help them, baby," Veronica said. She got up and stood back, giving me enough space to get out of the car, which I did without breaking eye contact.

"Mommy?" I softly whispered. I was worried I sounded pathetic but Veronica just smiled warmly and opened her arms to me.

"Come here baby, Mommy is here now," Veronica said and I almost burst into tears as I fell into her arms only to have them close tightly around me. She must have sensed my state of mind because she looked down and placed her hand on the side of my face, raising my eyes to meet hers.

"I'm going to look after you Hayley if you'd like that. I'd love to be your Mommy, not just for tonight, but for as long as you want me," Veronica said kissing the tip of my nose. I looked at her and smiled a smile of absolute submission. There was no way I could think of that would make me ever want to stop Veronica making me feel this way. She reached out her hand and I placed mine in hers, marveling at how even her hands were strong as she led me inside.

"Make yourself at home sweetie, I just need to get a few things," Veronica said as she disappeared. I wandered into the living room and sat awkwardly on the couch and waited for her to return. Coming back into the room, my eyes must have given me away because Veronica laughed and looked down.

"They aren't that exciting baby girl," she said talking about her comfortable house clothes. She was wearing a loose fitting t-shirt and a pair of long, gray, fluffy pajama pants. She came and sat next to me and I reached out to cuddle her involuntarily.

"Oh you are just the sweetest little one," Veronica said moving me onto her lap. I liked that she didn't mind me reaching for her I never wanted to let her go. We stayed like that, me on her lap, her stroking my arms and thighs until I could feel my eyes growing heavy.

"Come on little girl, Mommy needs to get you clean and out of your very beautiful but very grown-up clothes," Veronica said. I turned my head and looked at her, hoping that what I was about to say would be the right thing.

"Mommy, thank you," I said looking down and speaking so quietly it was almost a whisper. I felt Veronica envelop me and kiss me all over my face until I opened my eyes and giggled at her, pushing her away to make her stop.

"You're welcome, my little princess. Mommy knew what you needed then, and I guess fate bought us back together when we could be together and now little miss, you're Mommy's good girl," Veronica said standing me up and taking me to the bathroom.

"Strip for Mommy Hayley," Veronica said, reaching into her pants and starting to play with herself. I bit my bottom lip as I slowly pulled my dress off until I was standing in front of her with only my crimson lace thong and heels on. Veronica obviously liked what she saw because she reached out and took my hand, pulling me towards her and putting it down her pants. I could feel how wet she was instantly and gasped when she pulled my body into hers. She kissed me as I played with her pussy, enjoying teasing her and feeling her buck against my hand and grind down on it in frustration. She lifted me up and held me on her hip as I began to finger fuck her, giving her what I knew she wanted and she held me with one arm as the other pulled off her shirt. Taking her large breast in her hand she brought her nipple to my mouth and I instinctively took it, sucking and pulling on her nipple as I fucked her. Veronica moved so she was leaning against the wall as she came, holding me close and breathing deeply as the orgasm made her body shake and shudder. I felt her cum squirt out and cover my fingers and wrist, and dirty her pajama pants.

"Did you like that Mommy?" I giggled knowing full well she enjoyed herself. Veronica had shut her eyes but opened one and looked at me.

"Yes baby girl, you made Mommy very happy," Veronica said putting me back down. She took off her pants, and my panties and heels and ran us a bath.

"Do you want to bathe with Mommy tonight baby girl?" Veronica said making me clap my hands excitably.

"Yes please Mommy," I said wiggling my toes happily making Veronica smirk in satisfaction.

"Then come here and let Mommy help you in," Veronica instructed holding out a hand to me. I quickly took it and she held my hand firmly as I stepped into the warm soapy water. Sitting down in the tub I exhaled, closing my eyes and feeling calm for the first time in a long time.

"I was hoping you'd like this baby," Veronica said breaking the silence. I turned to see she had come into the bath and was sitting behind me. Pulling me into her, she held me by my neck and snaked her hand down my body to my clit, resting there before she cupped my pussy.

"Now Mommy is going to make you pay for teasing me earlier princess, do you really think I didn't know what you were doing my little minx?" Veronica whispered in my ear. I leaned back and felt her tits press into my should blades and neck as she began to part my pussy lips and entered me forcefully making me gasp and moan.

"I didn't say I'd be gentle did I baby girl. Mommy is going to force so many orgasms on you and there's nothing you can do about it. I'm going to love you through all of them, but Mommy isn't going to stop until you are limp in my arms precious baby," Veronica said as she held me in place and began pounding my pussy.

In what felt like no time at all I was squirming from left to right in the tub, splashing water onto the bathroom floor as Veronica forced the first orgasm on me.

"Shhh, little one, don't try and fight me, Mommy always wins," Veronica said as I panted and gasped at the intensity of my climax. I had never orgasmed so hard before and I was exhausted after the first one but Veronica wasn't joking when she said she wouldn't stop and didn't wait more than five seconds until she was fucking me under the water again.

"Mommy, I can't," I breathlessly tried to say as another orgasm took hold of me. I tighten my pussy trying to stop it from hitting so soon but Veronica just moved her fingers onto my clit and began rubbing me making me double over and grab her thighs as it ravaged my body. I loosened my grip and fell back into her as my body quivered and shook in the aftermath of her touch. I looked up at her with pleading eyes only to be met by her kisses.

"Give Mommy one more baby, I know you can give me one more," Veronica said making me nod my head. I wanted to give her whatever she wanted. I spread my legs and felt Veronica pat my pussy like she owned in and began rubbing me again. I wanted her nipple in my mouth again and pushed her hand away quickly and turned in her arms before she could get mad that I was denying her. I straddled her waist and kissed her deeply feeling her smile and bringing her hand back to force her fingers into me once again. I gasped and bent forward, feeling safe when Veronica placed her hand on my back.

"Come on baby girl, give it to Mommy," Veronica said patting my back and pressing her chest toward my mouth.

"Open your pretty mouth for Mommy," she instructed, rubbing her nipple across my lips. I began to suckle just as she began to slide her fingers in and out of my sensitive pussy. She must have felt how tender I was and this time let the orgasm build slowly, rubbing and stroking my clit tenderly, gently pushing and keeping her fingers inside of me as I began to moan.

"Please Mommy," I moaned making her quicken her pace. I wasn't sure how much longer I could take her slow onslaught but she held me close as my body fell limp on her lap. All too soon I began to cry and Veronica held me tenderly, wiping my tears away and telling me what a good girl I was until I was only snuggling into her neck.

"I have just never, felt that before," I said dropping my hand to play in the water.

"What sweetie?" Veronica asked.

"Kindness," I replied honestly, shifting on her lap to look at her. She smiled and kissed my forehead.

"I know. Will you let me love you a little longer?" Veronica asked. I sat back and ran my hands over her muscley shoulders and arms. I stopped at her abs and looked at her, smiling bashfully when she nodded her head for me to continue. I grabbed her full heavy breasts and traced over the ripples of her abs, stopping at her strong quads.

"I'll let you love me forever Mommy," I replied making her smile and splashing me playfully with the now cold water.

Mommy Will Take Care Of It

Savannah had lived by the beach for 3 years before she met Amber. Her life had been nothing special but she had a house by the beach and that suited her fine. She had a job at a local surf shop doing retail and had settled into a predictable, easy kind of life. The only thing Savannah had learned pretty quickly was that her new home didn't have the huge kink scene that had been available to her in the city. Out here, the kinkiest thing a girl had let her do was tie her down, and even that Savannah didn't find particularly thrilling. What she liked was being a Mommy to a sweet little baby girl. She liked to take them in and enjoy them for as long as they would let her. She'd give them baths and make them wear diapers, dress them in cute baby clothes and nurse them until their tummies were full. She would shower them in love and affection until for one reason or another, they'd leave.

"I just don't get it," Savannah said taking to her friend Josh on the phone.

"I just don't get how I can't keep a little baby. They always want you when they are sad but the minute life seems too easy for them, they are up and outa there. I hate it," Savannah explained. She had known Josh for years, meeting when they were both single but Josh had long since had a baby girl.

"I don't know, maybe you should be a bit more picky with who you spend your time with. I really wouldn't be so nice to them until they really show you that they want to be with you," Josh said. Savannah took his words to heart and vowed to make it difficult for the next girl to win her over.

"Hi, how may I help you?" Savannah said the next day to a girl how had brought in a broken board. Savannah hated the look of this girl the minute she saw her. She was just the type of girl who routinely broke Savannah's heart. With her tanned skin and sun-kissed face dotted with freckles, Savannah knew why her pulse began to race.

"I got the board home and realized that there was a chip in it, I was just wondering if I could exchange it for a new one?" The girl said. She had a surfers body, toned and lean with sun-bleached blonde hair, wavy from the sea salt. Savannah looked at the board and noticed that it was indeed chipped and hadn't been in the water yet.

"Yeah sure that's no problem, sorry about that. Let me just see if there's one out the back. Feel free to browse while I check," Savannah said. The girl smiled at her and Savannah wished she could take her out the back and fuck her until she couldn't walk but she just flicked through the boards until she found the right one.
Taking it back out onto the floor, the girl appeared from behind a shelf.

"Oh thanks, that's great," she said looking delighted. Savannah took her to the register and showed the girl where to fill out the paperwork for the exchange and was almost relieved when the girl left. However, that quickly turned into knowing dread when Savannah saw the message she had been left by the girl, 'Hey Savannah, I'm Amber - you already have my number X', Shit, thought Savannah, nervous that this would just lead to another heartbreak.

Savannah decided she would take Josh's advice and not jump into Amber's world head first. Instead, she had done the complete opposite and not messaged Amber at all trying to push her from her mind. A week after Amber had been in the store, Savannah looked up to see her walking in this time with a beach towel she had obviously bought previously.

"Hi, Amber," Savannah said making Amber smile.

"I didn't think you would remember me at all," Amber said raising an eyebrow. Savannah smirked, she sounds angry, she thought taking in Amber's attitude.

"Sorry I've just been really busy. What can I help you with this time?" Savannah said seeing her boss walk out the from the lunch room. Amber relaxed and placed the towel on the counter.

"I got this as a present but I think I'd like to exchange it for another color," Amber said. Savannah nodded and waited for Amber to turn and go look for what she wanted but she stayed at the counter and just looked blankly back at Savannah.

"Well, are you coming? I need your advice," Amber said blinking sweetly at Savannah. A familiar stirring began between Savannah's thighs and she smiled and came out from behind the counter.

"The towels are over here," Savannah said taking Amber's hand as she passed her and led her to the towels. Amber giggled and smiled up at Savannah who just rolled her eyes.

"Little girls like you honestly," Savannah said crossing her arms over her chest and watched Amber take 20 minutes to select a color she liked.

When she was finally ready to make the exchange Amber grabbed Savannah's forearm and stopped walking.

"What is it baby girl?" Savannah said involuntarily and held her breath hoping that Amber didn't mind.

"I was just wondering if there was a new one out the back?" Amber said, relieving Savannah's fears. Exhaling, Savannah relaxed and nodded turning toward the back room.

"Come with me," Savannah said and took Amber's hand once again. Amber giggled as Savannah pulled her into her the back room quickly, happy that it was a slow day and that no one else was in the store.

"This is naughty," Amber giggled. Savannah reached up and took down a new towel that still had its packaging on.

"Very naughty, do you know what I do with naughty girls Amber?" Savannah said, a winning smile widening on her face. Amber just shook her head no and held her towel to her chest. Savannah grabbed Amber's shoulder and spun her around making her face the shelving of the storeroom. Savannah lifted Amber's skirt and was greeted with light pink satin panties that made her moan.

"What a cute little girl you are," Savannah said trying to decide whether she was going to spank Amber and fuck her but as Amber wiggled her ass for Savannah, her hand came firmly down on Amber's ass making her drop her towel.

"Count them for me little one," Savannah said as she spanked Amber's panty covered ass.

"1, 2, 3, 4, 5, 6, ouch," Amber said breathlessly. Savannah stopped and rubbed Amber's reddening ass and grabbed her panties, pulling them up and into her ass making her cheeks bounce.

"That looks lovely my little slut, is that what you do, tease people until they play with you?" Savannah said, aware that she really needed to get back onto the main floor soon. Amber bit her bottom lip and just nodded, attempting to turn around and look at Savannah. Savannah placed her hand on Amber's head and turned her face away.

"Did I could say you could fucking look at me baby girl? I don't let naughty girls look at Mommy," Savannah said deciding she didn't care how Amber felt about the kink she was forcing on her. Amber just moaned and reached back to spread her ass for Savannah, making Savannah smile and wished she had more time to play with her. Giving Amber's ass one more spank, she took Amber's hands down and pulled her in for a cuddle.

"Come on baby, Mommy has to get back to work," Savannah whispered kissing her forehead before she grabbed the towel Amber had dropped and took her back out to the main floor. Turned on by the fact that she knew Amber's panties were still up her ass, Savannah wrote her number up Amber's arm and looked into her eyes as she spoke her parting words.

"If you don't call me within the hour, don't bother coming back," Savannah said in a low commanding voice, making sure no one else heard.

Amber just nodded, her wide eyes submitting to Savannah who just smiled and tilted her head to the door and Amber followed her instruction to leave.

Savannah finished her shift and checked her phone, hoping that Amber had followed her instruction and called her. Looking down Savannah was delighted to see that not only had Amber called and left a cute voice message, but had taken a series of photos and sent them as well. Ok, she likes me, thought Savannah as she happily flicked through the slutty photos Amber had sent her.

"Savannah? It's me, Amber," Amber said over the phone two weeks later. Savannah and Amber had seen each other a couple of times over the last two weeks and they had agreed to meet up tonight for a movie at a newly built cinema.

"Hi baby girl, are you OK?" Savannah replied, aware that they were met to meet up in a few hours. Amber sniffed and Savannah could tell that she had been crying.

"I don't think I'll be able to make it tonight, I'm getting kinda sick and I don't want you to get sick like me," Amber said getting teary again. Before Savannah could reply Amber spoke again.

"Sorry I get really emotional when I'm sick," Amber said melting Savannah's heart.

"It's OK baby girl can Mommy come over and make it all better?" Savannah asked hoping Amber would agree. She could tell Amber was smiling through the phone by her voice when she replied.

"Yes please Mommy, I thought you wouldn't want to because you might get sick," Amber said.

"Mommy has to make sure her baby girl is all better, I think I'll be fine, text me your address little girl," Savannah said, feeling her phone buzz with Amber's text.

"Alright baby, hold on, Mommy is on her way," Savannah said hanging up the phone and getting ready for a different kind of night.

Savannah arrived at Amber's house within the hour and was happy when she realized that Amber lived in a nice part of their beach town. She had ocean views and a little whitewashed wooden cottage on the top of a hill surrounded by a white picket fence and a gravel driveway. Cute, Savannah thought to herself as she got out and made her way to the front door. Before she could knock on the door, Amber opened it with a smile and a mug of tea. She sniffed and looked apologetically at Savannah.

"I'm sorry Mommy," Amber said as Savannah walked in and took the mug of tea from Amber's hands.

"It's OK, I guess Mommy has to look after you in more ways than just making sure you buy cute things," Savannah said realizing the tea was cold.

"Come on sweetie, let's get this sorted first," Savannah said gesturing to the tea.

Savannah made Amber a new pot of tea and ran

her a warm bath while they waited for the tea to slowly cool to drinking temperature. Undressing Amber, Savannah flicked her nipples until she squealed and pulled away.

"No," Savannah said waiting for Amber to move back to her previous position. Seeing that Amber wasn't sure what Savannah wanted, Savannah took her wrist and gently moved her onto the floor on her knees.

"Wider," Savannah said slapping Amber's thighs until she was satisfied.

"You're not so sick that you can't be in position for me baby girl, and this is how you'll wait for me when I say kneel, do you understand?" Savannah asked Amber who just nodded. Savannah clawed at Amber's tits until she whimpered.

"Say yes Mommy if you understand baby girl," Savannah said patiently and looked at the red marks she had made on Amber's soft flesh.

"Yes Mommy," Amber replied and Savannah moved Amber's hands onto the back of her head.

"Like this. Make sure Mommy doesn't have to repeat this lesson darling," Savannah said cupping Amber's chin and gently slapping her cheeks only stopping when her eyes began to water.

"Darling, you can let me know your limits," Savannah said hoping that Amber wasn't trying to be too brave.

"Ok Mommy, but it's OK, I'm just sensitive," Amber said looking up at Savannah who stood over her. Savannah pulled on Amber's nipples once again and enjoyed seeing them go hard and Amber bite her bottom lip trying not to break her position.

"Get in the bath little one," Savannah suddenly said, remembering that she was meant to be looking after Amber. Amber stood and Savannah helped her into the bath, poured her a tea and passed that to her next before beginning to pour warm water down Amber's back making low moans escape her throat.

"Do you like that baby girl?" Savannah asked and Amber began to nod before her eyes popped open as she remembered what Savannah wanted from her.

"Yes Mommy," Amber quickly said as Savannah bent down and kissed her forehead.

"Quick learner baby, you're going to make Mommy very happy," Savannah said as she began to rub between Amber's thighs.

"Don't get too excited, I'm not about to fuck you, little horny girl," Savannah laughed pulling the plug on Amber's bath before she was ready to get.

"But Mommy, don't you want to play with me?" Amber said letting Savannah dry her off. Savannah was drying Amber's feet and looked up at her with a menacing look.

"Careful what you ask for baby girl. You have no idea how badly I want to play with you but I'm not about to push you, not when you are sick," Savannah replied. Amber pouted before she clearly had an idea.

"But Mommy," Amber said, taking the towel from Savannah's hands and throwing it on the floor, turning around to face away from Savannah and spreading her ass cheeks showing Savannah her pussy and ass.

"Baby girl, don't tease Mommy," Savannah said, her last warning. Amber giggled and put two fingers in her mouth, sucking and licking them as Savannah crossed her arms and raised her eyebrow.

"Keep going little slut and Mommy will finish you," Savannah said watching Amber squat in front of her and slid her wet fingers into her pussy. Savannah grabbed Amber by her hair and lifted her to her feet.

"You asked for this little slut, Mommy is going to play with you the way I want to, you'd better not resist me," Savannah said dragging Amber to the living room and throwing her down on the couch. Amber turned around giggling but stopped as Savannah pulled her pants down and Amber's mouth was covered by Savannah's pussy.

"Worship me you little bitch, show Mommy why I should spend my time with you," Savannah moaned as Amber licked and sucked on Savannah's pussy. Savannah reached down and pushed two fingers into Amber's tight pussy and enjoyed hearing Amber gasp and groan as Savannah forced her fingers into her.

"Not so wet anymore are you baby girl, Mommy is going to fuck you raw until you are squirting for me," Savannah said and began pumping her fingers roughly in Amber, feeling Amber's panting breath on her pussy as her groans turned into moans and felt her hips buck trying to have Savannah deeper in her.

"Did I say stop bitch?" Savannah growled taking her fingers out of Amber and slapping her hand on her chest until Amber went back to eating Savannah out with an intensity she was satisfied with.

"Good, pretty little cunt, make Mommy happy," Savannah said as she felt her orgasm hit her covering Amber's mouth in her juices and clenched her thighs together making Amber swallow her cum.

"Drink me, bitch, what did Mommy say about resisting me?" Savannah said smiling as she felt Amber nervously begin to swallow her pussy juices.

Getting off Amber's face Savannah smiled as she saw Amber's wide-eyed submission and cum drenched chin and tits. Savannah rubbed her hands roughly over Amber's tits and slapped them roughly as she pulled Amber close and held her as she forced an orgasm on her.

"Mommy," Amber whimpered softly as she gripped Savannah's forearms and let her orgasm take her.

"Oh you are just a sweetheart aren't you baby girl," Savannah said happily seeing how wrecked Amber was after one orgasm.

"We can work on your stamina once you are better baby girl. Come on, let Mommy clean you again and get you into bed little one," Savannah said she took Amber back into the bathroom.

Mommy Is My Best Friend

"Candi," Mary called as she turned the key to her friend's apartment. Mary and Candice had been friends since they were in first grade. They had been in each other's classes all through school and when Mary went to Harvard for College, Candice made sure she was eligible for admittance as well. They had shared a dorm room until they both graduated with business degrees and had even started working for the same company. However, what Candice had never shared with Mary, not even once, was that she was a baby. A crayon coloring, diaper wearing, stuffie cuddling baby. She had loved the times Mary use to come home drunk from a frat party and cuddle in her bed with her or the way Mary would play with her hair, unknowingly putting her in her little space. But between College finishing and Mary's new boyfriend Cam, Candice knew that her cuddling days were numbered.

"I'm in here," Candice called back from the balcony. Tonight they were going to go out for one last girls night before Mary moved to the other side of the city with Cam. Candice hated Cam, not for any other reason except that he was the one person who had been able to take Mary away from her.

Mary appeared at the balcony and Candice had to catch her breath by what she saw. Mary had a leopard print wrap around dress that had a deep V neckline and a hem that stopped just under her ass. Her black high heels made the muscles in her strong thighs push out and I tightened my pussy trying to stay calm as she twirled in front of me.

"What do you think?" Mary asked bending down to kiss me on my cheek. I wish I hadn't blushed, I wished, even more, she hadn't of seen it.

"Oh you think I'm pretty, I knew you would, I might have dressed for you tonight," Mary teased taking my hand and placing it on her thigh. Pulling away I looked at her like she had lost her mind.

"Mary, what the fuck?" I asked almost angry that she was being so seductive tonight.

"Oh come on, you can't tell me that after all this time you haven't at least thought about it?" Mary replied grabbing my drink and finishing it. I shook my head and stood up, wanting to get away from her. Of course, I had thought about it. I'd thought about her in almost every possible position every night since we had been 14 but this was just too much. I couldn't even bring myself to look at her as she came in after me.

"Hey sorry I just thought it might be fun," Mary said softly. I looked up at her with tear-filled eyes and she pulled me in close to her.

"Candi, I'm sorry," Mary said stroking my hair. I held her, smelling her sweet perfume and letting her nurture me for the longest time before I broke the embrace.

"I've always thought about you, Mary. So doing this would just be too much knowing that you were moving away and that it wouldn't mean anything to you," I replied not daring to meet her eyes but I could tell she was frowning by the tone in her voice.

"It wouldn't mean nothing to me, you must know that I know," Mary said making me freeze. I looked at her and a shiver of terror shot down my body.

"What do you mean?" I replied hoping she wasn't about to say what I knew she was about to say.

"The blankie, all your excuses for coloring, the fact that you use to suck your thumb when we cuddled together Candi, I know," Mary explained making me burn red. I pushed her away and ran into my room, shutting the door behind me so Mary couldn't follow.

"Come on, don't be so silly," Mary yelled through the door. It was just all way too much. I couldn't believe she had known all this time. Oh how I had thought about her being my Mommy and here she was, willing, even teasing me to let her and I just couldn't. I stepped away from the door and Mary turned the handle, opening the door slightly.

"Will you let me come in?" She asked. I made a noise in my throat she knew to be yes and she walked in and shut the door behind her.

"Come and sit with me on your bed baby," Mary said making me open my mouth in protest.

"You don't have to do this Mary," I whispered, embarrassed. She smiled and opened her arms and I nervously walked over to her.

"You won't need these tonight," Mary said leaning down and taking off my heels. I let her, still rigid in her arms unable to relax. Feeling this, Mary began to open her dress.

"I know what the baby needs," Mary said pushing her breast into my mouth. I tried to resist her but she held me firmly and Mary had always been stronger than I was.

"Just suck baby girl, Mommy has been working on a special treat for you," Mary said forcing me to begin to regress. I could feel it coming, the little space she was pushing me into. As I was forced to suckle on her, I felt it, warm milk. My eyes grew wide and Mary smiled a toothy grin as I swallowed.

"There you go baby, drink up Mommy's milk," Mary said and just like that she had me. I stopped trying to push her away and relaxed into her arms, defeated but feeling very loved. Mary held me close as she began to rock me and loosened her grip, content that I wouldn't try to fight her anymore.

"Good girl. Mommy's clever little baby," Mary said patting my tummy. She held me for a few minutes longer before standing me up and taking off my black cocktail dress and bra. Stopping at my panties, Mary smiled.

"I have something I just know you're going to love baby girl," Mary said getting up and walking over to her bag. I hadn't seen it when she had come in, but she had brought over a big baby bag which I could see had a diaper poking out the top. Clapping my hands happily Mary laughed, coming back and bopping me on the head with a duck stuffie.

"Lie down for Mommy, let me dress you in something more appropriate baby girl," Mary said placing a changing mat on the floor. She guided me onto my back and I reached for the stuffie, excited to play with it.

"There you are baby girl, I told you Mommy had treats for you," Mary said sprinkling cold powder over me before sticking the diaper tabs down. Next, she took out a white cotton, long sleeve onesie and gently dressed me, clipping the onesies clips securely. Mary left me to play with the duck as she stood up and kicked her heels off. I liked seeing her settle in, knowing she wouldn't leave me.

"What shall we do tonight baby girl, I don't really think going out is on the table anymore," Mary asked sitting down on the couch. I looked up at her and thought about her question. I shrugged my shoulders and went back to playing making her laugh.

"Well if you have no ideas, then I guess you're at Mommy's mercy baby girl," Mary said spanking my ass making me giggle and try to crawl away from her. She grabbed my ankle and pulled me back to her. Mary held me in one arm as she began to rub herself under her dress.

"You didn't think Mommy would let you get away that easily did you, princess?" Mary asked taking my hand and sliding my fingers past her panties. I gasped, surprised how wet Mary was and she rolled her head back as I began to play with her.

"Don't you dare stop baby girl, make Mommy happy," Mary said slapping my face when I tried to pull my hand away. I pouted and looked at her but Mary just grabbed my hand and forced me to rub her harder. She reached over to her bag and pulled out a paddle and I pushed my fingers into her, not wanting her to use the paddle on me.

"Oh is someone scared baby girl?" Mary said bringing the paddle down on my diapered bottom hard enough for me to jump. I nodded my head and began sucking my thumb as my other hand finger fucked her.

"There is it little one, keep going," Mary said grabbing me and pulling me onto her lap as she was fucked. Using the paddle on my thighs and ass Mary began rocking against my hand and I felt her juices drip down my wrist as she came. Without warning, Mary got up and I fell on the floor with a thud.

"Get over here," Mary practically barked as she patted her lap. I stood up just to feel her paddle on my tummy.

"I said get over here, I never said to stand," Mary said as I dropped to my knees and she nodded encouragingly as I crawled to her.

"Better," Mary said grabbing my throat and pulling me onto her lap. I had always loved snuggling into Mary's thighs when we were at the beach or at the park having a picnic but she began touching me in a way she never had before.

"I wonder how much you can take little one," Mary said spanking me with all her strength, the paddle making a sound so loud I covered my ears.

"Cute little girl, take your hands away for Mommy," Mary said and waited while I nervously took my hands away. Mary paddled me until I was whimpering after each hit, the strength of her arm had me feeling the pain through my diaper. She held my head in her arm, bringing her breast to my mouth and let me suckle as she paddled me over and over.

"Mommy I can't," I whispered, worried that I was dangerously close to my limit. Mary smiled and squeezed milk into my mouth as she quickly paddled me hard and fast until I squealed and pulled away from her gasping.

"Good girl," Mary said slowly as she looked at me and put the paddle down. My ass was sore and felt red hot as Mary pulled me up and cuddled me again.

"I'm so impressed with you baby, you took so much more than I thought you could. My arm is even sore from the paddling you just took like such a good girl. Did Mommy hurt your little bottom?" Mary asked and took my thumb out of my mouth and replaced it with a purple paci. I nodded and she kissed my cheeks and forehead as she gently pushed me onto the floor and back onto the changing mat.

"Let Mommy see," Mary said slowly taking off me onesie and diaper. I could feel the burn of her paddle still on my ass and turned trying to see how red she had made me, resulting in her slapping my bare ass.

"Mommy," I said gasped in pain. Mary just slapped me a few more times, holding me in place as she had her way with me.

"It's not up to you sweetie," Mary said kindly as she kept slapping my sensitive skin making me whimper and moan.

"Shh, be a good girl for Mommy and take this," Mary said lovingly as she parted my ass cheeks and began rubbing my pussy.

"I knew you loved this Mommy's pretty little slut," Mary said slapping my ass harder in time to her rubbing my pussy. I didn't think I could last any longer and screamed as I came. I was mildly aware that Mary may have wanted me to ask permission but I couldn't think that thought through enough to get those words out. So I just lay there, spent and exhausted with Mary slapping my ass.

"You naughty girl, I didn't think I would have to spell everything out to you if you want to cum you ask Mommy for permission first little lady," Mary said.

That was the last thing I remember hearing but when I heard Mary's voice again, it wasn't the harsh tone she had used with me before.

"Baby girl, Mommy was so worried," Mary said. She had moved down to lay next to me and I blinked my eyes sleepily at her.

"If that was too much you should have said something darling," Mary said before she quickly corrected herself.

"I'm sorry Mommy didn't realize you needed to stop baby, did you push through so I would think you were a good girl?" Mary asked and cuddled me close when I nodded yes.

"Silly girl, Mommy will always think you are a good girl. I'm really proud of you baby, I won't take it that far again OK?" Mary said holding me gently in her arms. She let me bite her breasts before I tried to pull away from her.

"Where do you think you're going, Mommy has to take care of that little ass first baby," Mary said taking out lotion and laying me on my tummy as she rubbed the cool balm over my hot skin. It felt nice to have her take care of me and she kissed up my back when she was done.

"Let's get you dressed again darling," Mary said going to her bag and taking out a new diaper. She was gentle and soft as she lifted my body with ease and dressed me again before she picked me up and carried me into my bedroom. Placing me on the bed, she pulled back the sheets and cuddled with me.

"I don't want to lose you," I said burying my head into her ample chest.

"Baby girl, Cam is not the enemy. He

already has a little baby girl and boy, that's how I met him, I was looking for someone who understood all the things I wanted to do with you," Mary explained making my head swirl.

"I use to watch you while you slept. Stroked your hair out of your face and wrapped you in your blankie. I wanted you then, but I'm claiming you now. Are you really going to try and fight Mommy?" Mary asked. I curled my toes and pouted.

"But I don't want to share you, Mommy," I said saying Mommy for the first time. It made Mary beam that I had done so and she wrapped her arms around me making me feel safe and loved.

"I know you don't baby girl. How about this, from now on, you are Mommy's baby and we see each other once a week for playtimes. I'll stay over from Saturday Morning to Sunday lunchtime, what do you think?" Mary said. I nodded and clapped my hands happily. This had been my dream, to have Mary as my Mommy and now it had finally come true.

Who is Tina Moore?

Tina Moore has enjoyed the lifestyle of a Mommy Domme for several years. She began exploring kink and BDSM in her youth and found her love of being a strict Mommy Domme in early 2000. Tina Moore is now an author of many MDLG and ABDL themed novels.

Having enjoyed many years in the kink community, Tina Moore combines these experiences with the sweet and naughty things her baby girl does to bring you tantalizing and salacious stories.

Follow her on:

Author Page on Amazon

Instagram @tinamoore.kdp